Fantasmagoriana

(Tales of the Dead)

Edited & Introduced by A. J. Day
With translations by
A. J. Day & C. Vorwerk

First Published by Fantasmagoriana Press
St Ives, October 2005

First Edition

Copyright © A.J.Day 2004

Translations 'The ghost of the departed', 'The Grey Room' and 'The Black Chamber' © A.J.Day 2004
'Searching for the muse' © A.J.Day 2004

All rights reserved. No part of this publication may be reproduced, stored in or introduced into any retrieval system, or transmitted, in any form, or by any means (mechanical, electrical, photocopying, recording or otherwise) without the prior written permission of the author. Any person who commits any unauthorized act in relation to this publication may be liable to criminal prosecution and civil claims for damages.

10 9 8 7 6 5 4 3 2 1 0

This book is sold subject to the condition that it shall not, by way of trade or otherwise, be lent, re-sold, hired out, or otherwise circulated without the publisher's prior written consent in any form of binding or cover other than that in which it is published and without a similar condition including this condition being imposed on the subsequent purchaser.

To Nane

Acknowledgements

This book would not have been possible were it not for two people. I would like to thank my wife Christiane for her unwavering support and her assistance in the difficult and challenging task of translation. I am also indebted to Adelheid Vorwerk for her help in tracking down the original texts upon which much of this work rests.

The Spectre Barber (J. Masaus)   13

The Family Portraits (A. Apel)   37

The Fated Hour (F. Laun)   63

The Death Head (F. Laun)   77

The Death-Bride (F. Laun)   89

The Ghost of the Departed (F. Laun)   113

The Grey Room (H.C)   127

The Black Chamber (A. Apel)   137

Afterword (A.Day)   145

Introduction

'It was a dark and stormy night'.

'Although the gathering which ultimately resulted in Mary Shelley's writing of Frankenstein took place on the shores of Lake Geneva, mile from British soil, it must still qualify as one of the maddest British tea parties of all time.'
Stephen King

The original setting for the reading of *Fantasmagoriana* by an odd selection of English literati abroad was indeed upon a 'dark and stormy night'. It was undoubtedly the kind of conditions in which one should read ghost stories. Not surprising then, that it was also under such conditions that the idea of creating their own stories was thought of.

The atmosphere of the villa Diodati was charged by the violent streaks of lightening that licked at the mountain tops and split a black sky. As the wind outside whipped up the surface of lake Leman into a cauldron of waves the occupants of the Villa; Lord Byron, Mary Shelley, Dr John Polidori, Percy Shelley and Claire Clairmont whipped themselves into a gothic frenzy with recitals of haunting poetry and ghost stories.

If you are anything like the adventurous souls that have previously delighted in these tales then you are no doubt keen to get to the stories. As a result I have foregone a long and lengthy foreword that would only serve to distract from wonderful tales that lie within. Instead I have adopted a habit more common in the country from which the majority of these stories originate and have provided an in depth 'nachwort' or after-word. Here, parallels are drawn between elements of the stories read by the group and the text of Mary Shelley's *Frankenstein* in addition to looking deeper into other elements that may have been an influence upon Mary's first novel.

Reading the stories in *Fantasmagoriana* provided the inspiration for *Frankenstein* and, ultimately the sub-genre of horror and gothic literature within which the Vampyre lurks. This edition attempts to re-create, as accurately as possible, the original contents of the book that Lord Byron picked up from a bookseller in Geneva; a book that was to be instrumental in the conceiving of a work of English Literature that has remained in print for almost two hundred years.

The Spectre Barber

THERE had formerly lived at Bremen a wealthy merchant named Melchior, who, it was remarked, invariably stroked his chin with complacency, whenever the subject of the sermon was the rich man in the Gospel; who, by the bye, in comparison with him, was only a petty retail dealer. This said Melchior possessed such great riches, that he had caused the floor of his dining-room to be paved with crown-pieces. This ridiculous luxury gave great offence to Melchior's fellow-citizens and relations. They attributed it to vanity and ostentation, but did not guess its true motive: however, it perfectly answered the end Melchior designed by it; for, by their constantly expressing their disapprobation of this ostentatious species of vanity, they spread abroad the report of their neighbour's immense riches, and thereby augmented his credit in a most astonishing manner.

Melchior died suddenly while at a corporation dinner, and consequently had not time to make a disposition of his property by will; so that his only son Francis, who was just of age, came into possession of the whole. This young man was particularly favoured by fortune, both with respect to his personal advantages and his goodness of heart; but this immense inheritance caused his ruin, He had no sooner got into the possession of so considerable a fortune, than he squandered it, as if it had been a burthen to him; ran into every possible extravagance, and neglected his concerns. Two or three years passed over without his perceiving, that, owing to his dissipations, his funds were considerably diminished; but at length his coffers were emptied: and one day when Francis had drawn a draft to a very considerable amount on his banker, who had no funds to meet it, it was returned to him protested. This disappointment greatly vexed our prodigal, but only as it caused a temporary check to his wishes; for he did not even then give himself the trouble to inquire into the reason of it. After swearing and blustering for some time, he gave his steward a positive but laconic order to get money.

All the brokers, bankers, money-changers, and usurers, were put in requisition, and the empty coffers were soon filled; for the dining-room floor was in the eyes of the lenders a sufficient security.

This palliative had its effect for a time: but all at once a report was spread abroad in the city that the celebrated silver floor had been taken up; the consequence of which was, that the lenders insisted on examining into and proving the fact, and then became urgent for payment: but as Francis had not the means to meet their demands, they seized on all his goods and chattels; every thing was sold by auction, and he had nothing left excepting a few jewels which had formed part of his heritage, and which might for a short time keep him from starving.

He now took up his abode in a small street in one of the most remote quarters of the city, where he lived on his straitened means. He, however, accommodated himself to his situation: but the only resource he found against the *ennui* which overpowered him, was to play on the lute; and when fatigued by this exercise, he used to stand at his window and make observations on the weather; and his intelligent mind was not long in discovering an object which soon entirely engrossed his thoughts.

Opposite his window there lived a respectable woman, who was at her spinning-wheel from morning till night, and by her industry earned a subsistence for herself and her daughter. Meta was a young girl of great beauty and attraction: she had known happier times; for her father had been the proprietor of a vessel freighted by himself, in which he annually made trading voyages to Antwerp: but he, as well as his ship and all its cargo, was lost in a violent storm. His widow supported this double loss with resignation and firmness, and resolved to support herself and her daughter by her own industry. She made over her house and furniture to the creditors of her husband, and took up her abode in the little bye street in which Francis lodged, where by her assiduity she acquired a subsistence without laying herself under an obligation to any one. She brought up her daughter to spinning and other work, and lived with so much economy, that by her savings she was enabled to set up a little trade in linen.

Mother Bridget, (which was the appellation given to our widow,) did not, however, calculate on terminating her existence in this penurious situation; and the hope of better prospects sustained her courage. The beauty and excellent qualities of her daughter, whom she brought up with every possible care and attention, led her to think that some advantageous offer would one day present itself. Meta lived tranquilly and lonely with her mother, was never seen in any of the public walks, and indeed never went out but to mass once a day.

One day while Francis was making his meteorological observations at the window, he saw the beautiful Meta, who, under her mother's watchful eye, was returning from church. The heart of Francis was as yet quite free; for the boisterous pleasures of his past life did not leave him leisure for a true affection; but at this time, when all his senses were calm, the appearance of one of the most enchanting female forms he had ever seen, ravished him, and he henceforth thought solely of the adorable object which his eyes had thus discovered. He questioned his landlord respecting the two females who lived in the opposite house, and from him learned the particulars we have just related.

He now regretted his want of economy, since his present miserable state prevented him from making an offer to the charming Meta. He was, however, constantly at the window, in hopes of seeing her, and in that consisted his greatest delight. The mother very soon discovered the frequent appearance of her new neighbour at his window, and attributed it to its right cause. In consequence, she rigorously enjoined her daughter not to show herself at the windows, which were now kept constantly shut.

Francis was not much versed in the arts of finesse, but love awakened all the energies of his soul. He soon discovered that if he appeared much at the window, his views would be suspected, and he resolved therefore studiously to refrain from coming near it. He determined, however, to continue his observation of what occurred in the opposite dwelling without being perceived. He accordingly purchased a large mirror, and fixed it in his chamber in such a position that it distinctly presented to his view what passed in the abode of his opposite neighbour. Francis not being seen at the window, the old lady relaxed her rigour, and Meta's windows were once more opened. Love more than ever reigned triumphant in the bosom of Francis: but how was he to make known his attachment to its object? He could neither speak nor write to her. Love, however, soon suggested a mode of communication which succeeded. Our prodigal took his lute and drew from it tones the best adapted to express the subject of his passion; and by perseverance, in less than a month he made a wonderful progress. He soon had the gratification of seeing the fair hand of Meta open the little casement, when he began to tune the instrument. When she made her appearance, he testified his joy by an air lively and gay; but if she did not show herself, the melancholy softness of his tones discovered the disappointment he experienced.

In the course of a short time he created a great interest in the bosom of his fair neighbour; and various modes which love suggested shortly convinced our prodigal that Meta shared a mutual attachment. She now endeavoured to justify him, when her mother with acrimony spoke of his prodigality and past misconduct, by attributing his ruin to the effect of bad example. But in so doing, she cautiously avoided exciting the suspicions of the old lady; and seemed less anxious to excuse him, than to take a part in the conversation which was going on.

Circumstances which our limits will not allow us to narrate rendered the situation of Francis more and more difficult to be supported: his funds had now nearly failed him; and an offer of marriage from a wealthy brewer, who was called in the neighbourhood the 'King of Hops,' and which Meta, much to her mother's disappointment, refused, excited still more the apprehensions of poor Francis, lest some more fortunate suitor might yet be received, and blast his hopes for ever.

When he received the information that this opulent lover had been rejected for his sake, with what bitterness did he lament his past follies!

"Generous girl" said he, "you sacrifice yourself for a miserable creature, who has nothing but a heart fondly attached to you, and which is riven with despair that its possessor cannot offer you the happiness you so truly merit."

The King of Hops soon found another female, who listened more kindly to his vows, and whom he wedded with great splendour.

Love, however, did not leave his work incomplete; for its influence created in the mind of Francis a desire of exerting his faculties and actively employing himself, in order, if possible, to emerge from the state of nothingness into which he was at present plunged: and it inspired him also with courage to prosecute his good intentions. Among various projects which he formed, the most rational appeared that of overlooking his father's books, taking an account of the claimable debts, and from that source to get all he possibly could. The produce of this procedure would, he thought, furnish him with the means of beginning in some small way of business; and his imagination led him to extend this to the most remote corners of the earth. In order to equip himself for the prosecution of his plans, he sold all the remainder of his father's effects, and with the money purchased a horse to commence his travels.

The idea of a separation from Meta was almost more than he could endure. "What will she think," said he, "of this sudden disappearance, when she no longer meets me in her way to church? Will she not think me perfidious, and banish me from her heart?" Such ideas as these caused him infinite pain : and for a long while he could not devise any means of acquainting Meta with his plans; but at length the fertile genius of love furnished him with the following idea:- Francis went to the curate of the church which his mistress daily frequented, and requested him before the sermon and during mass to put up prayers for a *happy* issue *to the affairs of a young traveller;* and these prayers were to be continued till the moment of his return, when they were to be changed into those of thanks.

Every thing being arranged for his departure, he mounted his steed, and passed close under Meta's window. He saluted her with a very significant air, and with much less caution than heretofore. The young girl blushed deeply; and mother Bridget took this opportunity of loudly expressing her dislike to this bold adventurer, whose impertinence and foppery induced him to form designs on her daughter.

From this period the eyes of Meta in vain searched for Francis. She constantly heard the prayer which was put up for him; but was so entirely absorbed by grief at no longer perceiving the object of her affection, that she paid no attention to the words of the priest. In no way could she account for his disappearing. Some months afterwards, her grief being somewhat ameliorated, and her mind more tranquillized, when she was one day thinking of the last time she had seen Francis, the prayer arrested her attention; she reflected for an instant, and quickly divined for whom it was said; she naturally joined in it with great fervour, and strongly recommended the young traveller to the protection of her guardian angel.

Meanwhile Francis continued his journey, and had travelled the whole of a very sultry day over one of the desert cantons of Westphalia without meeting with a single house. As night approached, a violent storm came on: the rain fell in torrents; and poor Francis was soaked to the very skin. In this miserable situation he anxiously looked around, and fortunately discovered in the distance a light, towards which he directed his horse's steps; but as he drew near, he beheld a miserable cottage, which did not promise him much succour, for it more resembled a stable than the habitation of a human being. The unfeeling wretch who inhabited it refused him fire or water as if he had been a banished man - he was just about to extend himself on the straw in the midst of the cattle, and his indolence prevented his lighting a fire for the stranger. Francis vainly endeavoured to move the peasant to pity: the latter was inexorable, and blew out his candle with the greatest nonchalance possible, without bestowing a thought on Francis. However, as the traveller hindered him from sleeping, by his incessant lamentations and prayers, he was anxious to get rid of him.

"Friend," said he to him, "if you wish to be accommodated, I promise you it will not be here; but ride through the little wood to your left-hand, and you will find the castle belonging to the chevalier Eberhard Bronkhorst, who is very hospitable to travellers; but he has a singular mania, which is, to flagellate all whom he entertains: therefore decide accordingly."

Francis, after considering for some minutes what he had best do, resolved on hazarding the adventure. "In good faith," said he, "there is no great difference between having one's back broken by the miserable accommodation of a peasant, or by the chevalier Bronkhorst: friction disperses fever; possibly its effects may prove beneficial to me, if I am compelled to keep on my wet garments."

Accordingly he put spurs to his horse, and very shortly found himself before a gothic castle, at the Iron Gate of which he loudly knocked: and was answered from within by "Who's there?" But ere he was allowed time to reply, the gate was opened. However, in the first court he was compelled to wait with patience, till they could learn whether it was the lord of the castle's pleasure to flagellate a traveller, or send him out to pass the night under the canopy of heaven.

This lord of the castle had from his earliest infancy served in the Imperial army, under command of George of Frunsberg, and had himself led a company of infantry against the Venetians. At length, however, fatigued with warfare, he had retired to his own territory, where, in order to expiate the crimes he had committed during the several campaigns he had been in, he did all the good and charitable acts in his power. But his manner still preserved all the roughness of his former profession. The newly arrived guest, although disposed to submit to the usages of the house for the sake of the good fare, could not help feeling a certain trembling of fear as he heard the bolts grating, ere the doors were opened to him; and the very doors by their groaning noise seemed to presage the catastrophe which awaited him. A cold perspiration came over him as he passed the last door; but finding that he received the utmost attention, his fears a little abated. The servants assisted him in getting off his horse, and unfastened his cloak-bag; some of them led his horse to the stable, while others preceding him with flambeaux conducted Francis to their master, who awaited his arrival in a room magnificently lighted up.

Poor Francis was seized with an universal tremor when he beheld the martial air and athletic form of the lord of the castle, who came up to him and shook him by the hand with so much force that he could scarcely refrain from crying out, and in a thundering voice enough to stun him, told him he was welcome. Francis shook like an aspen leaf in every part of his body.

"What ails you, my young comrade?" cried the chevalier Bronkhorst, in his voice of thunder: "What makes you thus tremble, and renders you as pale as if death had actually seized you by the throat?"

Francis recovered himself; and knowing that his shoulders would pay the reckoning, his fears gave place to a species of audacity.

"My lord," answered he with confidence, "you see that I am so soaked with rain that one might suppose I had swam through the Weser; order me therefore some dry clothes instead of those I have on, and let us then drink a cup of hot wine, that I may, if possible, prevent the fever which otherwise may probably seize me. It will comfort my heart."

"Admirable!" replied the chevalier; "ask for whatever you want, and consider yourself here as at home."

Accordingly Francis gave his orders like a baron of high degree; he sent away the wet clothes, made choice of others, and, in fine, made himself quite at his ease. The chevalier, so far from expressing any dissatisfaction at his free and easy manners, commanded his people to execute whatever he ordered with promptitude, and condemned some of them as block-heads who did not appear to know how to wait on a stranger. As soon as the table was spread, the chevalier seated himself at it with his guest: they drank a cup of hot wine together.

"Do you wish for any thing to eat?" demanded the lord of Francis.

The latter desired he would order up what his house afforded, that he might see whether his kitchen was good.

No sooner had he said this, than the steward made his appearance, and soon furnished up a most delicious repast. Francis did not wait for his being requested to partake of it: but after having made a hearty meal, he said to the lord of the castle, "Your kitchen is by no means despicable; if your cellar is correspondent, I cannot but say you treat your guests nobly."

The chevalier made a sign to his butler, who brought up some inferior wine, and filled a large glass of it to his master, who drank to his guest. Francis instantly returned the compliment.

"Well, young man, what say you to my wine?" asked the chevalier.

" 'Faith," replied Francis, "I say it is bad, if it is the best you have in your cellar; but if you have none worse, I do not condemn it."

"You are a connoisseur;" answered the chevalier. "Butler, bring us a flask of older wine."

His orders being instantly attended to, Francis tasted it. "This is indeed some good old wine, and we will stick to it if you please."

The servants brought in a great pitcher of it, and the chevalier, being in high good-humour, drank freely with his guest; and then launched out into a long history of his several feats of prowess in the war against the Venetians. He became so overheated by the recital, that in his enthusiasm he overturned the bottles and glasses, and flourishing his knife as if it were a sword, passed it so near the nose and ears of Francis that he dreaded he should lose them in the action.

Though the night wore away, the chevalier did not manifest any desire to sleep; for he was quite in his element, whenever he got on the topic of the Venetian war. Each succeeding glass added to the heat of his imagination as he proceeded in his narration, till at length Francis began to apprehend that it was the prologue to the tragedy in which he was to play the principal part; and feeling anxious to learn whether he was to pass the night in the castle, or to be turned out, he asked for a last glass of wine to enable him to sleep well. He feared that they would commence by filling him with wine, and that if he did not consent to continue drinking, a pretext would be laid hold of for driving him out of the castle with the usual chastisement.

However, contrary to his expectation, the lord of the castle broke the thread of his narration, and said to him: "Good friend, every thing in its place: to-morrow we will resume our discourse."

"Excuse me, sir knight," replied Francis; "tomorrow, before sun-rise, I shall be on my road. The distance from hence to Brabant is very considerable, and I cannot tarry here longer, therefore permit me to take leave of you now, that I may not disturb you in the morning."

"Just as you please about that: but you will not leave the castle before I am up; we will breakfast together, and I shall accompany you to the outer gate, and take leave of you according to my usual custom."

Francis needed no comment to render these words intelligible. Most willingly would he have dispensed with the chevalier's company to the gate; but the latter did not appear at all inclined to deviate from his usual custom. He ordered his servants to assist the stranger in undressing, and to take care of him till he was in bed.

Francis found his bed an excellent one; and ere he went to sleep, he owned that so handsome a reception was not dearly bought at the expense of a trifling beating. The most delightful dreams (in which Meta bore the sway) occupied him the whole night; and he would have gone on (thus dreaming) till mid-day, if the sonorous voice of the chevalier and the clanking of his spurs had not disturbed him.

It needed all Francis's efforts to quit this delightful bed, in which he was so comfortable, and where he knew himself to be in safety: he turned from side to side; but the chevalier's tremendous voice was like a death-stroke to him, and at length he resolved to get up. Several servants assisted him in dressing, and the chevalier waited for him at a small but well-served table; but Francis, knowing the moment of trial was at hand, had no great inclination to feast. The chevalier tried to persuade him to eat, telling him it was the best thing to keep out the fog and damp air of the morning.

"Sir Knight," replied Francis, "my stomach is still loaded from your excellent supper, of last evening; but my pockets are empty, and I should much like to fill them, in order to provide against future wants."

The chevalier evinced his pleasure at his frankness by filling his pockets with as much as they could contain. As soon as they brought him his horse, which he discovered had been well groomed and fed, he drank the last glass of wine to say Adieu, expecting that at that signal the chevalier would take him by the collar and make him pay his welcome. But, to his no small surprise, the chevalier contented himself with heartily shaking him by the hand as on his arrival: and as soon as the gate was opened, Francis rode off safe and sound.

In no way could our traveller account for his host permitting him thus to depart without paying the usual score. At length he began to imagine that the peasant had simply told him the story to frighten him; and feeling a curiosity to learn whether or not it had any foundation in fact, he rode back to the castle. The chevalier had not yet quitted the gate, and was conversing with his servants on the pace of Francis's horse, who appeared to trot very roughly: and seeing the traveller return, he supposed that he had forgotten something and by his looks seemed to accuse his servants of negligence.

"What do you want, young man?" demanded he: "Why do you, who were so much pressed for time, return?"

"Allow me, most noble sir," replied Francis, "to ask you one question, for there are reports abroad which tend to vilify you: It is said, that, after having hospitably received and entertained strangers, you make them at their departure feel the weight of your arm. And although I gave credence to this rumour, I have omitted nothing which might have entitled me to this mark of your favour. But, strange to say, you have permitted me to depart in peace, without even the slightest mark of your strength. You see my surprise; therefore do pray inform me whether there is any foundation for the report, or whether I shall chastise the impudent story-teller who related the false tale to me."

"Young man," replied Bronkhorst, "you have heard nothing but the truth: but it needs some explanations. I open my door hospitably to every stranger, and in Christian charity I give them a place at my table; but I am a man who hates form or disguise; I say all I think, and only wish in return that my guests openly and undisguisedly ask for all they want. There are unfortunately, however, a tribe of people who fatigue by their mean complaisance and ceremonies without end; who wear me out by their dissimulation, and stun me by propositions devoid of sense, or who do not conduct themselves with decency during the repast. Gracious heavens! I lose all patience when they carry their fooleries to such excesses, and I exert my right as master of the castle, by taking hold of their collars, and giving them tolerably severe chastisement ere I turn them out of my gates. - But a man of your sort, my young friend, will ever be welcome under my roof; for you boldly and openly ask for what you require, and say what you think; and such are the persons I admire. If on your way back you pass through this canton, promise me you will pay me another visit. Good bye! Let me caution you never to place implicit confidence in any thing' you hear; believe only that there may be a single grain of truth in the whole story: be always frank, and you will succeed through life. Heaven's blessings attend you."

Francis continued his journey towards Anvers most gaily, wishing, as he went, that he might every where meet with as good a reception as at the chevalier Bronkhorst's.

Nothing remarkable occurred during the rest of his journey: and he entered the city full of the most sanguine hopes and expectations. In every street his fancied riches stared him in the face.

"It appears to me," said he, "that some of my father's debtors must have succeeded in business, and that they will only require my presence to repay their debts with honour."

After having rested from the fatigue of his journey, he made himself acquainted with every particular relative to the debtors, and learnt that the greater part had become rich, and were doing extremely well. This intelligence reanimated his hopes: he arranged his papers, and paid a visit to each of the persons who owed him any thing. But his success was by no means what he had expected: some of the debtors pretended that they had paid every thing; others, that they had never heard mention of Melchior of Bremen; and the rest produced accounts precisely contradictory to those he had, and which tended to prove they were creditors instead of debtors. In fine, ere three days had elapsed, Francis found himself in the debtors-prison, from whence he stood no chance of being released till he had paid the uttermost farthing of his father's debts.

How pitiable was this poor young man's condition! Even the horrors of the prison were augmented by the remembrance of Meta: - nay, to such a pitch of desperation was he carried, that he resolved to starve himself. Fortunately, however, at twenty-seven years of age such determinations are more easily formed than practised.

The intention of those who put him into confinement was not merely with a view of exacting payment of his pretended debts, but to avoid paying him his due: so, whether the prayers put up for poor Francis at Bremen were effectual, or that the pretended creditors were not disposed to maintain him during his life, I know not; but after a detention of three months they liberated Francis from prison, with a particular injunction to quit the territories of Anvers within four-and-twenty hours, and never to set his foot within that city again: - They gave him at the same time five florins to defray his expenses on the road. As one may well imagine, his horse and baggage had been sold to defray the costs incident to the proceedings.

With a heart overloaded with grief he quitted Anvers, in a very different frame of mind to what he experienced at entering it. Discouraged and irresolute, he mechanically followed the road which chance directed: he paid no attention to the various travellers, or indeed to any object on the road, till hunger or thirst caused him to lift his eyes to discover a steeple or some other token announcing the habitation of human beings. In this state of mind did he continue journeying on for several days incessantly; nevertheless a secret instinct impelled him to take the road leading to his own country.

All on a sudden he roused as if from a profound sleep, and recollected the place in which he was: he stopped an instant to consider whether he should continue the road he was then in, or return; "For," said he, "what a shame to return to my native city a beggar!" How could he thus return to that city in which he formerly felt equal to the richest of its inhabitants? How could he as a beggar present himself before Meta, without causing her to blush for the choice she had made? He did not allow time for his imagination to complete this miserable picture, for he instantly turned back, as if already he had found himself before the gates of Bremen, followed by the shouts of the children. His mind was soon made up as to what he should do: he resolved to go to one of the ports of the Low-Countries, there to engage himself as sailor on board a Spanish vessel, to go to the newly discovered world; and not to return to his native country till he had amassed as much wealth as he had formerly so thoughtlessly squandered. In the whole of this project, Meta was only thought of at an immeasurable distance: but Francis contented himself with connecting her in idea with his future plans, and walked, or rather strode along, as if by hurrying his pace he should sooner gain possession of her.

Having thus attained the frontiers of the Low-Countries, he arrived at sun-set in a village situated near Rheinburg; but since entirely destroyed in the thirty years' war. A caravan of carriers from Liege filled the inn so entirely, that the landlord told Francis he could not give him a lodging; adding, that at the adjoining village he would find accommodations. -Possibly he was actuated to this refusal by Francis's appearance, who certainly in point of garb might well be mistaken for a vagabond.

The landlord took him for a spy to a band of thieves, sent probably to rob the carriers: so that poor Francis, spite of his extreme lassitude, was compelled with his wallet at his back to proceed on his road; and having at his departure muttered through his teeth some bitter maledictions against the cruel and unfeeling landlord, the latter appeared touched with compassion for the poor stranger, and from the door of the inn called after him: "Young man; a word with you! If you resolve on passing the night here, I will procure you a lodging in that castle you now see on the hill; there you will have rooms in abundance, provided you are not afraid of being alone, for it is uninhabited. See, here are the keys belonging to it."

Francis joyfully accepted the landlord's proposition, and thanked him for it as if it had been an act of great charity.

"It is to me a matter of little moment where I pass the night, provided I am at my ease, and have something to eat." But the landlord was an ill-tempered fellow; and wishing to revenge the invectives Francis had poured forth against him, he sent him to the castle in order that he might be tormented by the spirits which were said to frequent it.

This castle was situated on a steep rock, and was only separated from the village by the high-road and a little rivulet. Its delightful prospects caused it to be kept in good repair, and to be well furnished, as its owner made use of it as a hunting-seat: but no sooner did night come on than he quitted it, in order to avoid the apparitions and ghosts which haunted it; but during the day nothing of the sort was visible, and all was tranquil.

When it was quite dark, Francis with a lantern in his hand proceeded towards the castle. The landlord accompanied him, and carried a little basket of provisions, to which he had added a bottle of wine (which he said would stand the test), as well as two candles and two wax-tapers for the night. Francis, not thinking he should require so many things, and being apprehensive he should have to pay for them, asked why they were all brought.

"The light from my lantern," said he, "will suffice me till the time of my getting into bed; and ere I shall get out of it, the sun will have risen, for I am quite worn out with fatigue."

"I will not endeavour to conceal from you," replied the landlord, "that according to the current reports this castle is haunted by evil spirits: but do not let that frighten you; you see I live sufficiently near, that, in case any thing extraordinary should happen to you, I can hear you call, and shall be in readiness with my people to render you any assistance. At my house there is somebody stirring all night, and there is also some one constantly on the watch. I have lived on this spot for thirty years, and cannot say that I have ever seen any thing to alarm me: indeed, I believe that you may with safety attribute any noises you hear during the night in this castle, to cats and weasels, with which the granaries are overrun. I have only provided you with the means of keeping up a light in case of need, for, at best, night is but a gloomy season; and, in addition, these candles are consecrated, and their light will undoubtedly keep off any evil spirits, should there be such in the castle."

The landlord spoke only the truth, when he said he had not seen any ghosts in the castle; for he never had the courage to set his foot within its doors after dark; and though he now spoke so courageously, the rogue would not have ventured on any account to enter. After having opened the door, he gave the basket into Francis's hand, pointed out the way he was to turn, and wished him good night: while the later, fully satisfied that the story of the ghosts must be fabulous, gaily entered. He recollected all that had been told him to the prejudice of the chevalier Bronkhorst, but unfortunately forgot what that brave Castellan had recommended to him at parting.

Conformably to the landlord's instructions, he went up stairs and came to a door, which the key in his possession soon unlocked: it opened into a long dark gallery, where his very steps re-echoed; this gallery led to a large hall, from which issued a suite of apartments furnished in a costly manner: he surveyed them all; and made choice of one in which to pass the night, that appeared rather more lively than the rest. The windows looked to the high-road, and every thing that passed in front of the inn could be distinctly heard from them. He lighted two candles, spread the cloth, ate very heartily, and felt completely at his ease so long as he was thus employed; for while eating, no thought or apprehension of spirits molested him but he no sooner arose from table, than he began to feel a sensation strongly resembling fear.

In order to render himself secure, he locked the door, drew the bolts, and looked out from each window; but nothing was to be seen. Every thing along the high-road and in front of the inn was tranquil, where, contrary to the landlord's assertions, not a single light was discernible. The sound of the horn belonging to the night-guard was the only thing that interrupted the silence which universally prevailed.

Francis closed the windows, once again looked round the room, and after snuffing the candles that they might burn the better, he threw himself on the bed, which he found good and comfortable: but although greatly fatigued, he could not get to sleep so soon as he had hoped. A slight palpitation of the heart, which he attributed to the agitation produced by the heat of his journey, kept him awake for a considerable time, till at length sleep came to his aid. After having as he imagined been asleep somewhat about an hour, he awoke and started up in a state of horror possibly not unusual to a person whose blood is overheated: this idea in some degree allayed his apprehensions; and he listened attentively, but could hear nothing excepting the clock, which struck the hour of midnight. Again he listened for an instant; and turning on his side, he was just going off to sleep again, when he fancied he heard a distant door grinding on its hinges, and then shut with a heavy noise. In an instant the idea of the ghost approaching caused him no little fear: but he speedily got the better of his alarm, by fancying it was only the wind; however, he could not comfort himself long with this idea, for the' sound approached nearer and nearer, and resembled the noise made by the clanking of chains, or the rattling of a large bunch of keys.

The terror which Francis experienced was beyond all description, and he put his head under the clothes. The doors continued to open wit] frightful noise, and at last he heard some one trying different keys at door of his room; one of them seemed perfectly to fit the lock, but bolts kept the door fast; however, a violent shock like a clap of thunder caused them to give way, and in stalked a tall thin figure with a black beard, whose appearance was indicative of chagrin and melancholy. He was habited in the antique style, and on his left shoulder wore a red cloak or mantle, while his head was covered with a high-crowned hat. Three times with slow and measured steps he walked round the room, examined the consecrated candles, and snuffed them: he then threw off his cloak, unfolded a shaving apparatus, and took from it the razors, which sharpened on a large leather strop hanging to his belt.

No powers are adequate to describe the agonies Francis endured: he recommended himself to the Virgin Mary, and endeavoured, as well as I fears would permit, to form an idea of the spectre's designs on him. Whether he purposed to cut his throat, or only take off his beard, he was at a loss to determine. The poor traveller, however, was a little more composed, when he saw the spectre take out a silver shaving-pot, and in a basin of the same metal put some water; after which he made a lather, and then placed a chair. But a cold perspiration came over Francis, when the spectre with a grave air, made signs for him to sit in that chair.

He knew it was useless to resist this mandate, which was but too plainly given: and thinking it most prudent to make a virtue of necessity, and put a good face on the matter, Francis obeyed the order, jumped nimbly out of bed, and seated himself as directed.

The spirit placed the shaving-bib round his neck: then taking a comb and scissors, cut off his hair and whiskers; after which he lathered according to rule, his beard, his eye-brows and head, and shaved them all off completely from his chin to the nape of his neck. This operatic ended, he washed his head, wiped and dried it very nicely, made him a low bow, folded up his case, put his cloak on his shoulder, and made towards the door to go away.

The consecrated candles had burnt most brilliantly during the whole this operation; and by their clear light Francis discovered, on looking at the glass, that he had not a single hair remaining on his head. More bitterly did he deplore the loss of his beautiful brown hair: but he regained courage on remarking, that, however great the sacrifice, all was now over and that the spirit had no more power over him.

In effect, the ghost walked towards the door with as grave an air as he had entered: but after going a few steps, he stopped, looked at Francis with a mournful air, and stroked his beard. He three times repeated this action; and was on the point of quitting the room, when Francis began to fancy he wanted something. With great quickness of thought he imagined it might be, that he wished him to perform a like service for him to that which he had just been executing on himself.

As the spectre, spite of his woe-begone aspect, appeared more inclined to raillery than gravity, and as his proceedings towards Francis appeared more a species of frolic than absolute ill treatment, the latter no longer appeared to entertain any apprehension of him; and in consequence determined to hazard the adventure. He therefore beckoned the phantom to seat himself in the chair. It instantly returned, and obeyed: taking off its cloak, and unfolding the case, it placed it on the table, and seated itself in the chair, in the attitude of one about to be shaved. Francis imitated precisely all he had seen it do: he cut off its hair and whiskers, and then lathered its head. The spirit did not move an inch. Our barber's apprentice did not handle the razor very dexterously; so that having taken hold of the ghost's beard against the grain, the latter made a horrible grimace. Francis did not feel much assured by this action: however, he got through the job as well as he could, and rendered the ghost's head as completely bald as his own.

Hitherto the scene between the two performers had passed in profound silence; but on a sudden the silence was interrupted by the ghost exclaiming with a smiling countenance: - "Stranger, I heartily thank you for the eminent service you have rendered me; for to you am I indebted for deliverance from my long captivity. During the space of three hundred years I have been immersed within these walls, and my soul has been condemned to submit to this chastisement as a punishment for my crimes, until some living being had the courage to exercise retaliation on me, by doing to me what I have done by others during my life.

"Count Hartmann formerly resided in this Castle: he was a man who recognized no law nor superior; was of an arrogant and overbearing disposition; committed every species of wickedness, and violated the most sacred rights of hospitality: he played all sorts of malicious tricks to strangers who sought refuge under his roof, and to the poor who solicited his charity. I was his barber, and did every thing to please him. No sooner did I perceive a pious pilgrim, than in an endearing tone I urged him to come into the castle, and prepared a bath for him; and while he was enjoying the idea of be mg taken care of, I shaved his beard and head quite close, and then turned him out of the bye door, with raillery and ridicule. All this was seen by count Hartmann from his window with a sort of devilish pleasure, while the children would assemble round the abused stranger, and pursue him with cries of derision.

"One day there came a holy man from a far distant country; he wore a penitentiary cross at his back, and his devotion had imprinted scars on his feet, hands, and sides; his head was shaved, excepting a circle of hair left to resemble the crown of thorns worn by our Saviour. He asked some water to wash his feet as he passed by, and some bread to eat. I instantly put him into the bath; but did not respect even *his* venerable head. Upon which the pilgrim pronounced this terrible curse on me: 'Depraved wretch,' said he, 'know that at your death, the formidable gates of heaven, of hell, and of purgatory will alike be closed against your sinful soul, which shall wander through this castle, in the form of a ghost, until some man, without being invited or constrained, shall do to you, what you have so long done to others.'

"From that moment the marrow in my bones dried up, and I became a perfect shadow; my soul quitted my emaciated body, and remained wandering within these walls, according to the prediction of the holy man. In vain did I look and hope for release from the painful ties which held me to earth; for know, that no sooner is the soul separated from the body, than it aspires to the blissful regions of peace, and the ardour of its wishes causes years to appear as long as centuries, while it languishes in a strange element. As a punishment, I am compelled to continue the trade that I had exercised during my life; but, alas! My nocturnal appearance soon rendered this castle deserted. Now and then a poor pilgrim entered to pass the night here: when they did, however, I treated them all as I have done you; but not one has understood me, or rendered me the only service which could deliver my soul from this sad servitude. Henceforth no spirit will haunt this castle; for I shall now enjoy that repose of which I have been so long in search. Once again let me thank you, gallant youth; and believe, that had I power over the hidden treasures of the globe, I would give them all to you; but, unfortunately, during my life riches did not fall to my lot, and this castle contains no store: however, listen to the advice I am now about to give you.

"Remain here till your hair has grown again; then return to your own country; and at that period of the year when the days and nights are of equal length, go on the bridge which crosses the Weser, and there remain till a friend, whom you will there meet, shall tell you what you ought to do to get possession of terrestrial wealth. When you are rolling in riches and prosperity, remember me; and on every anniversary of the day on which you released me from the heavy maledictions which overwhelmed me, cause a mass to be said for the repose of my soul. Adieu! I must now leave you."

Thus saying, the phantom vanished, and left his liberator perfectly astonished at the strange history he had just related. For a considerable time Francis remained immoveable and reasoned with himself as to the reality of what he had seen; for he could not help fancying still that it was only a dream: but his closely shaved head soon convinced him that the event had actually taken place. He got into bed again, and slept soundly till mid-day.

The malicious inn-keeper had been on the watch from dawn of day for the appearance of the traveller, in order that he might enjoy a laugh at his expense, and express his surprise at the night's adventure. But after waiting till his patience was nearly exhausted, and finding it approached to noon, he began to apprehend that the spirit had either strangled the stranger, or that he had died of fright. He therefore called his servants together, and ran with them to the castle, passing through every room till he reached the one in which he had observed the light the over-night: there he found a strange key in the door, which was still bolted; for Francis had drawn the bolts again after the ghost had vanished. The landlord, who was all anxiety, knocked loudly; and Francis on awaking, at first thought it was the phantom come to pay him a second visit; but at length recognizing the landlord's voice, he got up and opened the door.

The landlord, affecting the utmost possible astonishment, clasped his hands together, and exclaimed, "Great God and all the saints! Then the *red cloak* has actually been here and shaved you completely? I now see that the story was but too well founded. But pray relate to me all the particulars: tell me what the spirit was like; how he came thus to shave you; and what he said to you?"

Francis, having sense enough to discover his roguery, answered him by saying: "The spirit resembled a man wearing a red cloak; you know full well how he performed the operation: and his conversation I perfectly remember; - listen attentively: - 'Stranger,' said he to me, 'do not trust to a certain inn-keeper who has a figure of malice for his sign; the rogue knew well what would happen to you. Adieu! I now quit this abode, as my time is come; and in future no spirit will make its appearance here. I am now about to be transformed into a nightmare, and shall constantly torment and haunt this said inn-keeper, unless he does penance for his villainy, by lodging, feeding, and furnishing you with every thing needful, till your hair shall grow again and fall in ringlets over your shoulders.' "

At these words the landlord was seized with a violent trembling: he crossed himself, and vowed to the Virgin Mary that he would take care of the young stranger, lodge him, and give him every thing he required free of cost. He then conducted him to his house, and faithfully fulfilled what he promised.

The spirit being no longer heard or seen, Francis was naturally looked on as a conjuror. He several times passed a night in the castle; and one evening a courageous villager accompanied him, and returned without having lost his hair. The lord of the castle, hearing that the formidable *red cloak* was no longer to be seen, was quite delighted, and gave orders that the stranger who had delivered him from this spirit should be well taken care of.

Early in the month of September, Francis's hair began to form into ringlets, and he prepared to depart; for all his thoughts were directed towards the bridge over the Weser, where he hoped, according to the barber's predictions, to find the friend who would point out to him the way to make his fortune.

When Francis took leave of the landlord, the latter presented him with a handsome horse well appointed, and loaded with a large cloak-bag on the back of the saddle, and gave him at the same time a sufficient sum of money to complete his journey. This was a present from the lord of the castle, expressive of his thanks for having delivered him from the spirit, and rendered his castle again habitable.

Francis arrived at his native place in high spirits. He returned to his lodging in the little street, where he lived very retired, contenting himself for the present with secret information respecting Meta. All the tidings he thus gained were of a satisfactory nature; but he would neither visit her, nor make her acquainted with his return, till his fate was decided.

He waited with the utmost impatience for the equinox; till which, time seemed immeasurably long. The night preceding the eventful day, he could not close his eyes to sleep; and that he might be sure of not missing the friend with whom as yet he was unacquainted, he took his station ere sun-rise on the bridge, where no human being but himself was to be discovered. Replete with hopes of future good fortune, he formed a thousand projects in what way to spend his money.

Already had he, during the space of nearly an hour, traversed the bridge alone, giving full scope to his imagination; when on a sudden the bridge presented a moving scene, and amongst others, many beggars took their several stations on it, to levy contributions on the passengers. The first of this tribe who asked charity of Francis was a poor devil with a wooden leg, who, being a pretty good physiognomist, judged from the gay and contented air of the young man that his request would be crowned with success; and his conjecture was not erroneous, for he threw a demi-florin into his hat Francis, meanwhile, feeling persuaded that the friend he expected must belong to the highest class of society, was not surprised at not seeing him at so early an hour, and waited therefore with patience. But as the hour for visiting the Exchange and the Courts of justice drew near, his eyes were in constant motion. He discovered at an immense distance every well-dressed person who came on the bridge, and his blood was in a perfect ferment as each approached him, for in some one of them did he hope to discover the author of his good fortune; but it was in vain his looking the people in the face, no one paid attention to him. The beggars, who at noon were seated on the ground eating their dinner, remarking that the young man they had seen from the first of the morning was the only person remaining with them on the bridge, and that he had not spoken to any one, or appeared to have any employment, took him for a lazy vagabond; and although they had received marks of his beneficence, they began to make game of him, and in derision called him the *provost* of the bridge. The physiognomist with the wooden leg remarked that his air was no longer so gay as in the morning, and that having drawn his hat over his face he appeared entirely lost in thought, for he walked slowly along, nibbling an apple with an abstracted air. The observer, resolving to benefit by what he had remarked, went to the further extremity of the bridge, and after well examining the visionary, came up to him as a stranger, asked his charity, and succeeded to his utmost wish; for Francis, without turning round his head, gave him another demi-florin.

In the afternoon a crowd of new faces presented themselves to Francis's observation, while he became quite weary at his friend's tardiness; but hope still kept up his attention. However, the fast declining sun gave notice of the approach of night, and yet scarcely any of the many passersby had noticed Francis. Some few, perhaps, had returned his salutation, but not one had, as he expected and hoped, embraced him. At length, the day so visibly declined that the bridge became nearly deserted; for even the beggars went away. A profound melancholy seized the heart of poor Francis, when he found his hopes thus deceived; and giving way to despair, he would have precipitated himself into the Weser, had not the recollection of Meta deterred him. He felt anxious, ere he terminated his days in so tragical a manner, to see her once again as she went to mass, and feast on the contemplation of her features.

He was preparing to quit the bridge, when the beggar with the wooden leg accosted him, for he had in vain puzzled his brains to discover what could possibly have caused the young man to remain on the bridge from morning till night. The poor cripple had waited longer than usual on account of Francis, in order to see when he went; but as he remained longer than he wished, curiosity at length induced him openly to address him, in order to learn what he so ardently desired to know.

"Pray excuse me, worthy sir," said he; "and permit me to ask you a question."

Francis, who was by no means in a mood to talk, and who now heard from the mouth of a beggar the words which he had so anxiously expected from a friend, answered him in rather an angry tone: "Well then! What is it you want to know, old man?"

"Sir, you and I were the two first persons on this bridge to-day; and here we are still the only remaining two. As for me and my companions, it is pretty clear that we only come to ask alms: but it is equally evident you do not belong to our profession; and yet you have not quitted the bridge the whole day. My dear Sir, for the love of God, if it is no secret, tell me I entreat you for what purpose you came, and what is the grief that rends your heart?"

"What can it concern you, old dotard, to know where the shoe pinches me, or what afflictions I am labouring under?"

"My good sir, I wish you well; you have twice bestowed your charity on me, which I hope the Almighty will return to you with interest. I could not but observe, however, that this evening your countenance no longer looked gay and happy as in the morning; and, believe me, I was sorry to see the change."

The unaffected interest evinced by the old man pleased Francis.

"Well," replied he, "since you attach so much importance to the knowledge of the reason I have for remaining the whole day here plaguing myself, I will inform you that I came in search of a friend who appointed to meet me on this bridge, but whom I have expected in vain."

"With your permission I should say your friend is a rogue, to play the fool with you in this manner. If he had so served *me,* I should make him feel the weight of my crutch whenever I met him: for if he has been prevented from keeping his word by any unforeseen obstacle, he ought at least to have sent to you, and not have kept you here on your feet a whole day."

"And yet I have no reason to complain of his not coming, for he promised me nothing. In fact, it was only in a dream that I was told I should meet a friend here."

Francis spoke of it as a dream, because the history of the ghost was too long to relate.

"That alters the case," replied the old man. "Since you rest your hopes on dreams, I am not astonished at your being deceived. I have also had many dreams in my life; but I was never fool enough to pay attention to them. If I had all the treasures that have been promised me in dreams, I could purchase the whole city of Bremen: but I have never put faith in dreams, and have not taken a single step to prove whether they were true or false; for I know full well, it would be useless trouble: and I am astonished that you should have lost so fine a day, which you might have employed so much more usefully, merely on the strength of a dream, which appears to me so wholly devoid of sense or meaning."

"The event proves the justness of your remark, old father; and that dreams generally are deceitful. But it is rather more than three months since I had a very circumstantial dream relative to my meeting a friend on this particular day, here on this bridge; and it was so clearly indicated that he should communicate things of the utmost importance, that I thought it worth while to ascertain whether this dream had any foundation in truth."

"Ah! Sir, no one has had clearer dreams than myself; and one of them, I shall never forget. I dreamt, several years since, that my good angel stood at the foot of my bed, in the form of a young man, and addressed me as follows:- 'Berthold, listen attentively to my words, and do not lose any part of what I am about to say. A treasure is allotted you; go and secure it, that you may be enabled to live happily the rest of your days. Tomorrow evening, when the sun is setting, take a pick-axe and spade over your shoulder, and go out of the city by the gate leading to Hamburgh: when you arrive facing the convent of Saint Nicholas, you will see a garden, the entrance to which is ornamented by two pillars; conceal yourself behind one of these until the moon rises: then push the door hard, and it will yield to your efforts; go without fear into the garden, follow a walk covered by a treillage of vines, and to the left you will see a great apple tree: place yourself at the foot of this tree, with your face turned towards the moon, and you will perceive, at fifteen feet distance, two bushy rose-trees: search between these two shrubs, and at the depth of about six feet you will discover a great flag-stone, which covers the treasure enclosed within an iron chest; and although it is heavy and difficult to handle, do not regret the labour it will occasion you to move it from the hole where it now is. You will be well rewarded for your pains and trouble, if you look for the key which is hid under the box.'"

Francis remained like one stupefied at this recital; and certainly would have been unable to conceal his astonishment, if the darkness of the night had not favoured him. The various particulars pointed out by the beggar brought to his recollection a little garden which he had inherited from his father, and which garden was the favourite spot of that good man; but possibly for that very reason it was not held in estimation by the son. Melchior had caused it to be laid out according to his own taste, and his son in the height of his extravagance had sold it at a very low price.

The beggar with his wooden leg was now become a very interesting personage to Francis, who perceived that he was the friend alluded to by the ghost in the castle of Rummelsbourg. The first impulse of joy would have led him to embrace the mendicant; but he restrained his feelings, thinking it best not to communicate the result of his intelligence to him.

"Well, my good man," said he, "what did you when you awoke? Did you not attend to the advice given by your good angel?"

"Why should I undertake a hopeless labour? It was only a vague dream; and if my good angel was anxious to appear to me, he might choose a night when I am not sleeping, which occurs but too frequently: but he has not troubled his head much about me; for if he had, I should not have been reduced, as I now am, to his shame, to beg my bread."

Francis took from his pocket another piece of money, and gave it to the old man, saying: "Take this to procure half a pint of wine, and drink it ere you retire to rest. Your conversation has dispelled my sorrowful thoughts; do not fail to come regularly to this bridge, where I hope we shall meet again."

The old lame man, not having for a long while made so good a day's work, overwhelmed Francis with his grateful benedictions. They separated, and each went their way. Francis, whose joy was at its height from the near prospect of his hopes being realised, very speedily reached his lodging in the bye street.

The following day he ran to the purchaser of the little garden, and proposed to re-purchase it. The latter, to whom this property was of no particular value, and indeed who began to be tired of it, willingly consented to part with it. They very soon agreed as to the conditions of the purchase, and went immediately to sign the contract: with the money he had found in his bag, as a gift from the lord of Rummelsbourg, Francis paid down half the price: he then procured the necessary tools for digging a hole in the earth, conveyed them to the garden, waited till the moon was up, strictly adhered to the instructions given him by the old beggar, set to work, and without any unlucky adventure he obtained the hidden treasure.

His father, as a precaution against necessity, had buried this money, without any intention to deprive his son of this considerable portion of his inheritance; but dying suddenly, he had carried the secret to his grave, and nothing but a happy combination of circumstances could have restored this lost treasure to its rightful owner.

The chest filled with gold pieces was too heavy for Francis to remove to his lodging without employing some person to assist him: and feeling unwilling to become a topic of general conversation, he preferred concealing it in the summer-house belonging to the garden, and fetching it at several times. On the third day the whole was safely conveyed to his lodging in the little back street.

Francis dressed himself in the best possible style, and went to the church to request that the priest would substitute for the prayers which had been previously offered up, a thanksgiving *for the safe return of a traveller to his native country, after having happily terminated his business.* He concealed himself in a corner, where, unseen, he could observe Meta. The sight of her gave him inexpressible delight, especially when he saw the beautiful blush which overspread her cheeks, and the brilliancy of her eyes, when the priest offered up the thanksgiving. A secret meeting took place as had been formerly arranged; and so much was Meta affected by it, that any indifferent person might have divined the cause.

Francis repaired to the Exchange, set up again in business, and in a very short time had enough to do; his fortune each succeeding day becoming better known, his neighbours judged that he had had greater luck than sense in his journey to collect his father's debts. He hired a large house in the best part of the town, engaged clerks, and continued his business with laudable and indefatigable assiduity; he conducted himself with the utmost propriety and sagacity, and abstained from the foolish extravagancies which had formerly been his ruin. The re-establishment of Francis's fortune formed the general topic of conversation. Every one was astonished at the success of his foreign voyage: but in proportion to the spreading fame of his riches, did Meta's tranquillity and happiness diminish; for it appeared that her silent lover was now in a condition to declare himself openly, and yet he remained dumb, and only manifested his love by the usual rencontre on coming out of church; and even this species of rendezvous became less frequent, which appeared to evince a diminution of his affection.

Poor Meta's heart was now torn by jealousy; for she imagined that the inconstant Francis was offering up his vows to some other beauty. She had experienced secret transports of delight on learning the change of fortune of the man she loved, not from interested motives and the wish to participate in his bettered fortune herself, but from affection to her mother, who, since the failure of the match with the rich brewer, absolutely seemed to despair of ever enjoying happiness or comfort in this world. When she thought Francis faithless, she wished that the prayers put up for him in the church had not been heard, and that his journey had not been attended with such entire success; for had he been reduced to means merely sufficient to procure the necessaries of life, in all probability he would have shared them with her.

Mother Bridget failed not to perceive her daughter's uneasiness, and easily guessed the cause; for she had heard of her old neighbour's surprising return, and she knew he was now considered an industrious intelligent merchant; therefore she thought if his love for her daughter was what it ought to be, he would not be thus tardy in declaring it; for she well knew Meta's sentiments towards him. However, feeling anxious to avoid the probability of wounding her daughter's feelings, she avoided mentioning the subject to her: but the latter, no longer able to confine her grief to her own bosom, disclosed it to her mother, and confided the whole to her.

Mother Bridget did not reproach her daughter for her past conduct, but employed all her eloquence to console her, and entreated her to bear up with courage under the loss of all her hopes:

"You must resign him," said she: "you scorned at the happiness which presented itself to your acceptance, therefore you must now endeavour to be resigned at its departure. Experience has taught me that those hopes which appear the best founded are frequently the most delusive; follow my example, and never again deliver up your heart. Do not reckon on any amelioration of your condition, and you will be contented with your lot. Honour this spinning-wheel which produces the means of your subsistence, and then fortune and riches will be immaterial to you: you may do with out them."

Thus saying, mother Bridget turned her wheel round with redoubled velocity, in order to make up for the time lost in conversation. She spoke nothing but the truth to her daughter: for since the opportunity was gone by when she hoped it was possible to have regained her lost comforts, she had in such a manner simplified her present wants and projects of future life, that it was not in the power of destiny to produce any considerable derangement in them. But as yet Meta was not so great a philosopher so that her Mother's exhortations, consolations, and doctrines, produced a precisely different effect on her from what they were intended. Meta looked on herself as the destroyer of the flattering hopes her mother had entertained. Although she did not formerly accept the offer of marriage proposed to her, and even then could not have reckoned on possessing beyond the common necessaries of life; yet, since she had heard the tidings of the great fortune obtained by the man of her heart, her views had become enlarged, and she anticipated with pleasure that by her choice she might realize her mother's wishes.

Now, however, this golden dream had vanished: Francis would not come again; and indeed they even began to talk in the city of an alliance about to take place between him and a very rich young lady of Anvers. This news was a death-blow to poor Meta: she vowed she would banish him from her thoughts; but still moistened her work with her tears.

Contrary, however, to her vow, she was one day thinking of the faithless one: for whenever she filled her spinning-wheel, she thought of the following distich, which her mother had frequently repeated to her to encourage her in her work: "Spin the thread well; spin, spin it more, for see your intended is now at the door."

Some one did in reality knock gently at the door; and mother Bridget went to see who it was. Francis entered, attired as for the celebration of a wedding. Surprise, for a while, suspended mother Bridget's faculties of speech. Meta, blushing deeply and trembling, arose from her seat, but was equally unable with her mother to say a word. Francis was the only one of the three who could speak; and he candidly declared his love, and demanded of Bridget the hand of her daughter. The good mother, ever attentive to forms, asked eight days to consider the matter, although the tears of joy which she shed, plainly evinced her ready and prompt acquiescence: but Francis, all impatience, would not hear of delay: finding which, she, conformable to her duty as a mother, and willing to satisfy Francis's ardour, adopted a mid-way, and left the decision to her daughter. The latter, obeying the dictates of her heart, placed herself by the side of the object of her tenderest affection; and Francis, transported with joy, thanked her by a kiss.

The two lovers then entertained themselves with talking over the delights of the time when they so well communicated their sentiments by signs. Francis had great difficulty in tearing himself away from Meta and such 'converse sweet,' but he had an important duty to fulfil.

He directed his steps towards the bridge over the Weser, where he hoped to find his old friend with the wooden leg, whom he had by no means forgotten, although he had delayed making the promised visit. The latter instantly recognised Francis; and no sooner saw him at the foot of the bridge, than he came to meet him, and shewed evident marks of pleasure at sight of him.

"Can you, my friend," said Francis to him, after returning his salutation, "come with me into the new town and execute a commission? You will be well rewarded for your trouble."

"Why not? - with my wooden leg, I walk about just as well as other people; and indeed have an advantage over them, for it is never fatigued. I beg you, however, my good sir, to have the kindness to wait till the man with the grey great-coat arrives."

"What has this man in the grey great-coat to do with you?"

"He every day comes as evening approaches and gives me a demi-florin; I know not from whom. It is not indeed always proper to learn all things; so I do not breathe a word. I am sometimes tempted to believe, that it is the devil who is anxious to buy my soul; but it matters little, I have not consented to the bargain, therefore it cannot be valid."

"I verily believe that grey surtout has some malice in his head; so follow me, and you shall have a quarter-florin over and above the bargain."

Francis conducted the old man to a distant corner, near the ramparts of the city, stopped before a newly built house, and knocked at the door. As soon as the door was opened, he thus addressed the old beggar: "You have procured a very agreeable evening for me in the course of my life; it is but just, therefore, that I should shed some comforts over your declining days. This house and every thing appertaining thereto belongs to you. The kitchen and cellar are both well stocked; there is a person to take care of you, and every day at dinner you will find a quarter-florin under your plate. It is now time for you to know that the man in the grey surtout is my servant, whom I every day sent with my alms till this house was ready to receive you. You may, if you please, consider me as your guardian angel, since your good angel did not acquit himself uprightly in return for your gratitude."

Saying this, he made the old man go in to his house; where the latter found every thing he could possibly desire or want. The table was spread; and the old man was so much astonished at this unexpected good fortune, that he thought it must be a dream; for he could not in any way imagine why a rich man should feel so much interest for a miserable beggar. Francis having again assured him that every thing he saw was his own, a torrent of tears expressed his thanks; and before he could sufficiently recover from his astonishment to express his gratitude by words, Francis had vanished.

The following day, mother Bridget's house was filled with merchants and shopkeepers of all descriptions, whom Francis had sent to Meta, in order that she might purchase and get ready every thing she required for her appearance in the world with suitable *éclat.* Three weeks afterwards he conducted her to the altar. The splendour of the wedding far exceeded that of the *King of* Hops. Mother Bridget enjoyed the satisfaction of adorning her daughter's forehead with the nuptial crown, and thereby obtained the accomplishment of all her desires, and was recompensed for her virtuous and active life. She witnessed her daughter's happiness with delight, and proved the very best of grand-mothers to her daughter's children.

The Family Portraits

Night had insensibly superseded day, when Ferdinand's carriage continued its slow course through the forest; the postilion uttering a thousand complaints on the badness of the roads, and Ferdinand employing the leisure which the tedious progress of his carriage allowed, with reflections to which the purpose of his journey gave rise.

As was usual with young men of rank, he had visited several universities; and after having traveled over the principal parts of Europe, he was now returning to his native country to take possession of the property of his father, who had died in his absence.

Ferdinand was an only son, and the last branch of the ancient family of Meltheim: it was on this account that his mother was the more anxious that he should form a brilliant alliance, to which both his birth and fortune entitled him; she frequently repeated that Clotilde of Mainthal was of all others the person she should be most rejoiced to have as a daughter-in-law, and who should give to the world an heir to the name and estates of Meltheim. In the first instance, she merely named her amongst other distinguished females whom she recommended to her son's attention: but after a short period she spoke of none but her: and at length declared, rather positively, that all her happiness depended on the completion of this alliance, and hoped her son would approve her choice.

Ferdinand, however, never thought of this union but with regret; and the urgent remonstrances which his mother ceased not to make on the subject, only contributed to render Clotilde, who was an entire stranger to him, less amiable in his eyes: he determined at last to take a journey to the capital, whither Mr. Hainthal and his daughter were attracted by the carnival. He wished at least to know the lady, ere he consented to listen to his mother's entreaties; and secretly flattered himself that he should find some more cogent reasons for opposing this union than mere caprice, which was the appellation the old lady gave to his repugnance.

Whilst travelling alone in his carriage, as night approached, the solitary forest, his imagination drew a picture of his early life, which happy recollections rendered still happier. It seemed, that the future presented no charms for him to equal the past; and the greater pleasure he took in retracing what no longer existed, the less wish he felt to bestow a thought on that futurity to which, contrary to his inclinations, he seemed destined. Thus, notwithstanding the slowness with which his carriage proceeded over the rugged ground, he found that he was too rapidly approaching the termination of his journey.

The postilion at length began to console himself; for one half of the journey was accomplished, and the remainder presented only good roads: Ferdinand, however, gave orders to his groom to stop at the approaching village, determining to pass the night there.

The road through the village which led to the inn was bordered by gardens, and the sound of different musical instruments led Ferdinand to suppose that the villagers were celebrating some rural fête. He already anticipated the pleasure of joining them, and hoped that this recreation would dissipate his melancholy thoughts. But on listening more attentively, he remarked that the music did not resemble that usually heard at inns; and the great light he perceived at the window of a pretty house from whence came the sounds that had arrested his attention, did not permit him to doubt that a more select party than are accustomed to reside in the country at that unfavourable season, were amusing themselves in performing a concert.

The carriage now stopped at the door of a small inn of mean appearance. Ferdinand, who counted on much inconvenience and few comforts, asked who was the lord of the village. They informed him that he occupied a *château* situated in an adjoining hamlet. Our traveller said no more, but was obliged to content himself with the best apartment the landlord could give him. To divert his thoughts, he determined to walk in the village, and directed his steps towards the spot where he had heard the music; to this the harmonious sounds readily guided him : he approached softly, and found himself close to the house where the concert was performing. A young girl, sitting at the door, was playing with a little dog, who began to bark. Ferdinand, drawn from his reverie by this singular accompaniment, begged the little girl to inform him who lived in that house.

"It is my father," she replied, smiling; "come in, sir." And saying this, she slowly went up the steps.

Ferdinand hesitated for an instant whether to accept this unceremonious invitation. But the master of the house came down, saying to him in a friendly tone:

"Our music, sir, has probably been the only attraction to this spot; no matter, it is the pastor's abode, and to it you are heartily welcome. My neighbours and I," continued he, whilst leading Ferdinand in, "meet alternately at each other's houses once a week, to form a little concert; and to-day it is my turn. Will you take a part in the performance, or only listen to it? Sit down in this apartment. Are you accustomed to hear better music than that performed simply by amateurs? or do you prefer an assemblage where they pass their time in conversation? If you like the latter, go into the adjoining room, where you will find my wife surrounded by a young circle: here is our musical party, there is their conversation."

Saying this, he opened the door, made a gentle inclination of the head to Ferdinand, and seated himself before his desk. Our traveller would fain have made apologies; but the performers in an instant resumed the piece he had interrupted. At the same time the pastor's wife, a young and pretty woman, entreated Ferdinand, in the most gracious manner possible, entirely to follow his own inclinations, whether they led him to remain with the musicians, or to join the circle assembled in the other apartment. Ferdinand, after uttering some commonplace terms of politeness, followed her into the adjoining room.

The chairs formed a semicircle round the sofa, and were occupied by several women and by some men. They all rose on Ferdinand's entering, and appeared a little disconcerted at the interruption. In the middle of the circle was a tow chair, on which sat, with her back to the door, a young and sprightly female, who, seeing every one rise, changed her position, and at sight of a stranger blushed and appeared embarrassed. Ferdinand entreated the company not to interrupt the conversation. They accordingly reseated themselves, and the mistress of the house invited the new guest to take a seat on the sofa by two elderly ladies, and drew her chair near him.

"The music," she said to him, "drew you amongst us, and yet in this apartment we have none; I hear it nevertheless with pleasure myself: but I cannot participate in my husband's enthusiasm for simple quartets and symphonies; several of my friends are of the same way of thinking with me, which is the reason that, while our husbands are occupied with their favourite science, we here enjoy social converse, which sometimes, however, becomes too loud for our *virtuoso* neighbours. Today, I give a long-promised tea-drinking. Every one is to relate a story of ghosts, or something of a similar nature. You see that my auditors are more numerous than the band of musicians."

"Permit me, madam," replied Ferdinand, "to add to the number of your auditors; although I have not much talent in explaining the marvellous."

"That will not be any hindrance to you here," answered a very pretty brunette; "for it is agreed amongst us that no one shall search for any explanation, even though it bears the stamp of truth, as explanations would take away all pleasure from ghost stories."

"I shall benefit by your instructions," answered Ferdinand: "but without doubt I interrupt a very interesting recital; - dare I entreat - ?"

The young lady with flaxen hair, who rose from the little seat, blushed anew; but the mistress of the house drew her by the arm, and laughing, conducted her to the middle of the circle.

"Come, child," said she, "don't make any grimace; reseat yourself, and relate your story. This gentleman will also give us his."

"Do you promise to give us one, sir?" said the young lady to Ferdinand. He replied by a low bow. She then reseated herself in the place destined for the narrator, and thus began:

"One of my youthful friends, named Juliana, passed every summer with her family at her father's estate. The *château* was situated in a romantic country; high mountains formed a circle in the distance; forests of oaks and fine groves surrounded it. It was an ancient edifice, and had descended through a long line of ancestry to Juliana's father; for which reason, instead of making any alterations, he was only anxious to preserve it in the same state they had left it to him.

"Among the number of antiquities most prized by him was the family picture gallery; a vaulted room, dark, high, and of gothic architecture, where hung the portraits of his forefathers, as large as the natural size, covering the walls, which were blackened by age. Conformable to an immemorial custom, they ate in this room and Juliana has often told me, that she could not overcome, especially at supper-time, a degree of fear and repugnance; and that she had frequently feigned indisposition, to avoid entering this formidable apartment. Among the portraits there was one of a female, who, it would seem, did not belong to the family; for Juliana's father could neither tell whom it represented, nor how it had become ranged amongst his ancestry: but as to all appearance it had retained its station for ages, my friend's father was unwilling to remove it.

"Juliana never looked at this portrait without an involuntary shuddering and she has told me, that from her earliest infancy she has felt this secret terror, without being able to define the cause. Her father treated this sentiment as puerile, and compelled her sometimes to remain alone in that room. But as Juliana grew up, the terror this singular portrait occasioned, increased; and she frequently supplicated her father, with tears in her eyes, not to leave her alone in that apartment – 'That portrait,' she would say, 'regards me not gloomily or terribly, but with looks full of a mild melancholy. It appears anxious to draw me to it, and as if the lips were about to open and speak to me. - That picture will certainly cause my death.'

"Juliana's father at length relinquished all hope of conquering his daughter's fears. One night at supper, the terror she felt had thrown her into convulsions, for she fancied she saw the picture move its lips; and the physician enjoined her father in future to remove from her view all similar causes of fear. In consequence, the terrifying portrait was removed from the gallery, and it was placed over the door of an uninhabited room in the attic story.

"Juliana, after this removal, passed two years without experiencing any alarms. Her complexion resumed its brilliancy, which surprised every one; for her continual fears had rendered her pale and wan: but the portrait and the fears it produced had alike disappeared, and Juliana –"

"Well," cried the mistress of the house, smiling, when she perceived that the narrator appeared to hesitate, "confess it, my dear child; Juliana found an admirer of her beauty; - was it not so?"

"Tis even so," resumed the young lady, blushing deeply; "she was affianced: and her intended husband coming to see her the day previous to that fixed on for her marriage, she conducted him over the *chateau,* and from the attic rooms was shewing him the beautiful prospect which extended to the distant mountains. On a sudden she found herself, without being aware of it, in the room where the unfortunate portrait was placed. And it was natural that a stranger, surprised at seeing it there alone, should ask who it represented. To look at it, recognise it, utter a piercing shriek, and run towards the door, were but the work of an instant with poor Juliana. But whether in effect owing to the violence with which she opened the door the picture was shaken, or whether the moment was arrived in which its baneful influence was to be exercised over Juliana, I know not; but at the moment this unfortunate girl was striving to get out of the room and avoid her destiny, the portrait fell; and Juliana, thrown down by her fears, and overpowered by the heavy weight of the picture, never rose more. –"

A long silence followed this recital, which was only interrupted by the exclamations of surprise and interest excited for the unfortunate Juliana. Ferdinand alone appeared untouched by the general emotions. At length, one of the ladies sitting near him broke the silence by saying, "This story is literally true; I knew the family where the fatal portrait caused the death of a charming young girl: I have also seen the picture; it has, as the young lady truly observed, an indescribable air of goodness which penetrates the heart, so that I could not bear to look on it long; and yet, as you say, its look is so full of tender melancholy, and has such infinite attractions, that it appears that the eyes move and have life."

"In general," resumed the mistress of the house, at the same time shuddering, "I don't like portraits, and I would not have any in the rooms I occupy. They say that they become pale when the original expires; and the more faithful the likeness, the more they remind me of those waxen figures I cannot look at without aversion."

"That is the reason," replied the young person who had related the history, "that I prefer those portraits where the individual is represented occupied in some employment, as then the figure is entirely independent of those who look at it; whereas in a simple portrait the eyes are inanimately fixed on every thing that passes. Such portraits appear to me as contrary to the laws of illusion as painted statues."

"I participate in your opinion," replied Ferdinand; "for the remembrance of a terrible impression produced on my mind when young, by a portrait of that sort, will never be effaced."

"O! pray relate it to us," said the young lady with flaxen hair, who had not as yet quitted the low chair; "you are obliged according to promise to take my place." She instantly arose, and jokingly forced Ferdinand to change seats with her.

"This history," said he, "will resemble a little too much the one you have just related; permit me therefore –"

"That does not signify," resumed the mistress of the house, "one is never weary with recitals of this kind; and the greater repugnance I feel in looking at these horrible portraits, the greater is the pleasure I take in listening to histories of their eyes or feet being seen to move."

"But seriously," replied Ferdinand, who would fain have retracted his promise, "my history is too horrible for so fine an evening. I confess to you that I cannot think of it without shuddering, although several years have elapsed since it happened."

"So much the better, so much the better!" cried nearly all present; "how you excite our curiosity! And its having happened to yourself will afford double pleasure, as we cannot entertain any doubt of the fact."

"It did not happen personally to me," answered Ferdinand, who reflected that he had gone too far, "but to one of my friends, on whose word I have as firm a reliance as if I had been myself a witness to it."

They reiterated their entreaties; and Ferdinand began in these words:-

"One day, when I was arguing with the friend of whom I am about to make mention, on apparitions and omens, he told me the following story;-

" 'I had been invited,' said he, 'by one of my college companions, to pass my vacations with him at an estate of his father's. The spring was that year unusually late, owing to a long and severe winter, and appeared in consequence more gay and agreeable, which gave additional charms to our projected pleasures. We arrived at his father's in the pleasant month of April, animated by all the gaiety the season inspired.

"As my companion and I were accustomed to live together at the university, he had recommended to his family, in his letters, so to arrange matters that we might live together at his father's also: we in consequence occupied two adjoining rooms, from whence we enjoyed a view of the garden and a fine country, bounded in the distance by forests and vineyards. In a few days I found myself so completely at home in the house, and so familiarised with its inhabitants, that nobody, whether of the family or among the domestics, made any difference between my friend and myself. His younger brothers, who were absent from me in the day, often passed the night in my room or in that of their elder brother. Their sister, a charming girl about twelve years of age, lovely and blooming as a newly blown rose, gave me the appellation of brother, and fancied that under this title she was privileged to shew me all her favourite haunts in the garden, to gratify my wishes at table, and to furnish my apartment with all that was requisite. Her cares and attention will never be effaced from my recollection; they will long outlive the scenes of horror that chateau never ceases to recall to my recollection. From the first of my arrival, I had remarked a huge portrait affixed to the wall of an antechamber through which I was obliged to pass to go to my room; but, too much occupied by the new objects which on all sides attracted my attention, I had not particularly examined it. Meanwhile, I could not avoid observing that, though the two younger brothers of my friend were so much attached to me, that they would never permit me to go at night into my room without them, yet they always evinced an unaccountable dread in crossing the hall where this picture hung. They clung to me, and embraced me that I might take them in my arms; and whichever I was compelled to take by the hand, invariably covered his face, in order that he might not see the least trace of the portrait.

"Being aware that the generality of children are afraid of colossal figures, or even of those of a natural height, I endeavoured to give my two young friends courage. However, on more attentively considering the portrait which caused them so much dread, I could not avoid feeling a degree of fear myself. The picture represented a knight in the costume of a very remote period; a full grey mantle descended from his shoulders to his knees; one of his feet placed in the foreground, appeared as if it was starting from the canvass; his countenance had an expression which petrified me with fear. I had never before seen any thing at all like it in nature. It was a frightful mixture of the stillness of death, with the remains of a violent and baneful passion, which not even death itself was able to overcome. One would have thought the artist had copied the terrible features of one risen from the grave, in order to paint this terrific portrait. I was seized with a terror little less than the children, whenever I wished to contemplate this picture. Its aspect was disagreeable to my friend, but did not cause him any terror: his sister was the only one who could look at this hideous figure with a smiling countenance; and said to me with a compassionate air, when I discovered my aversion to it, 'That man is not wicked, but he is certainly very unhappy.' My friend told me that the picture represented the founder of his race, and that his father attached uncommon value to it; it had, in all probability, hung there from time immemorial, and it would not be possible to remove it from this chamber without destroying the regularity of its appearance.

"Meanwhile, the term of our vacation was speedily drawing to its close, and time insensibly wore away in the pleasures of the country. The old count, who remarked our reluctance to quit him, his amiable family, his *château*, and the fine country that surrounded it, applied himself with kind and unremitting care, to make the day preceding our departure a continual succession of rustic diversions: each succeeded the other without the slightest appearance of art; they seemed of necessity to follow each other. The delight that illumined the eyes of my friend's sister when she perceived her father's satisfaction; the joy that was painted in Emily's countenance (which was the name of this charming girl) when she surprised even her father by her arrangements, which outstripped his projects, led me to discover the entire confidence that existed between the father and daughter, and the active part Emily had taken in directing the order which reigned in that day's festivities.

"Night arrived; the company in the gardens dispersed; but my amiable companions never quitted my side. The two young boys skipped gaily before us, chasing the may-bug, and shaking the shrubs to make them come out. The dew arose, and aided by the light of the moon formed silver spangles on the flowers and grass. Emily hung on my arm; and an affectionate sister conducted me, as if to take leave, to all the groves and places I had been accustomed to visit with her, or with the family. On arriving at the door of the chateau, I was obliged to repeat the promise I had made to her father, of passing some weeks in the autumn with him. 'That season,' said she, 'is equally beautiful with the spring!' With what pleasure did I promise to decline all other engagements for this. Emily retired to her apartment, and, according to custom, I went up to mine, accompanied by my two little boys: they ran gaily up the stairs; and in crossing the range of apartments but faintly lighted, to my no small surprise their boisterous mirth was not interrupted by the terrible portrait.

"For my own part, my head and heart were full of the intended journey, and of the agreeable manner in which my time had passed at the count's *chateau*. The images of those happy days crowded on my recollection; my imagination, at that time possessing all the vivacity of youth, was so much agitated, that I could not enjoy the sleep which already overpowered my friend. Emily's image, so interesting by her sprightly grace, by her pure affection for me, was present to my mind like an amiable phantom shining in beauty. I placed myself at the window, to take another look at the country I had so frequently ranged with her, and traced our steps again probably for the last time. I remembered each spot illumined by the pale light the moon afforded. The nightingale was singing in the groves where we had delighted to repose; the little river on which while gaily singing we often sailed, rolled murmuringly her silver waves.

"Absorbed in a profound reverie, I mentally exclaimed: With the flowers of spring, this soft pure peaceful affection will probably fade; and as frequently the after seasons blight the blossoms and destroy the promised fruit, so possibly may the approaching autumn envelop in cold reserve that heart which, at the present moment, appears only to expand with mine!

"Saddened by these reflections, I withdrew from the window, and overcome by a painful agitation I traversed the adjoining rooms; and on a sudden found myself before the portrait of my friend's ancestor. The moon's beams darted on it in the most singular manner possible, insomuch as to give the appearance of a horrible moving spectre; and the reflection of the light gave to it the appearance of a real substance about to quit the darkness by which it was surrounded. The inanimation of its features appeared to give place to the most profound melancholy; the sad and glazed look of the eyes appeared the only hindrance to its uttering its grief.

"My knees tremblingly knocked against each other, and with an unsteady step I regained my chamber: the window still remained open; I reseated myself at it, in order that the freshness of the night air, and the aspect of the beautiful surrounding country, might dissipate the terror I had experienced. My wandering eyes fixed on a long vista of ancient linden trees, which extended from my window to the ruins of an old tower, which had often been the scene of our pleasures and rural fêtes. The remembrance of the hideous portrait had vanished; when on a sudden there appeared to me a thick fog issuing from the ruined tower, which advancing through the vista of lindens came towards me.

"I regarded this cloud with an anxious curiosity: it approached; but again it was concealed by the thickly spreading branches of the trees.

"On a sudden I perceived, in a spot of the avenue less dark than the rest, the same figure represented in the formidable picture, enveloped in the grey mantle I so well knew. It advanced towards the *chateau,* as if hesitating: no noise was heard of its footsteps on the pavement; it passed before my window without looking up, and gained a back door which led to the apartments in the colonnade of the *chateau.*

"Seized with trembling apprehension, I darted towards my bed, and saw with pleasure that the two children were fast asleep on either side. The noise I made awoke them; they started, but in an instant were asleep again. The agitation I had endured took from me the power of sleep, and I turned to awake one of the children to talk with me: but no powers can depict the horrors I endured when I saw the frightful figure at the side of the child's bed.

"I was petrified with horror, and dared neither move nor shut my eyes. I beheld the spectre stoop towards the child and softly kiss his forehead: he then went round the bed, and kissed the forehead of the other boy.

"I lost all recollection at that moment; and the following morning, when the children awoke me with their caresses, I was willing to consider the whole as a dream.

"Meanwhile, the moment for our departure was at hand. We once again breakfasted all together in a grove of lilacs and flowers. 'I advise you to take a little more care of yourself,' said the old count in the midst of other conversation; 'for I last night saw you walking rather late in the garden, in a dress ill suited to the damp air; and I was fearful such imprudence would expose you to cold and fever. Young people are apt to fancy they are invulnerable; but I repeat to you, Take advice from a friend.'

" 'In truth,' I answered, 'I believe readily that *I* have been attacked by a violent fever, for never before was I so harassed by terrifying visions: I can now conceive how dreams afford to a heated imagination subjects for the most extraordinary stories of apparitions.

" 'What would you tell me?' demanded the count in a manner not wholly devoid of agitation. I related to him all that I had seen the preceding night; and to my great surprise he appeared to me in no way astonished, but extremely affected.

" 'You say,' added he in a trembling voice, 'that the phantom kissed the two children's foreheads?' I answered him that it was even so. He then exclaimed, in accents of the deepest despair, 'Oh heavens! they must then both die!' " -

Till now the company had listened without the slightest noise or interruption to Ferdinand: but as he pronounced the last words, the greater part of his audience trembled; and the young lady who had previously occupied the chair on which he sat, uttered a piercing shriek.

"Imagine," continued Ferdinand, "how astonished my friend must have been at this unexpected exclamation. The vision of the night had caused him excess of agitation; but the melancholy voice of the count pierced his heart, and seemed to annihilate his being, by the terrifying conviction of the existence of the spiritual world, and the secret horrors with which this idea was accompanied. It was not then a dream, a chimera, the fruit of an over-heated imagination! but a mysterious and infallible messenger, which, dispatched from the world of spirits, had passed close to him, had placed itself by his couch, and by its fatal kiss had dropt the germ of death in the bosom of the two children."

"He vainly entreated the count to explain this extraordinary event. Equally fruitless were his son's endeavours to obtain from the count the development of this mystery, which apparently concerned the whole family. 'You are as yet too young,' replied the count: 'too soon, alas! for your peace of mind, will you be informed of these terrible circumstances which you now think mysterious.

"Just as they came to announce to my friend that all was ready, he recollected that during the recital the count had sent away Emily and her two younger brothers. Deeply agitated, he took leave of the count and the two young children who came towards him, and who would scarcely permit themselves to be separated from him. Emily, who had placed herself at a window, made a sign of adieu. Three days afterwards the young count received news of the death of his two younger brothers. They were both taken off in the same night.

"You see," continued Ferdinand, in a gayer tone, in order to counteract the impression of sadness and melancholy his story had produced on the company; "You see my history is very far from affording any natural explication of the wonders it contains; explanations which only tend to shock one's reason: it does not even make you entirely acquainted with the mysterious person, which one has a right to expect in all marvellous recitals. But *I* could learn nothing more; and the old count dying without revealing the mystery to his son, I see no other means of terminating the history of the portrait, which is undoubtedly by no means devoid of interest, than by inventing according to one's fancy a denouement which shall explain all."

"That does not appear at all necessary to me," said a young man: "this history, like the one that preceded it, is in reality finished, and gives all the satisfaction one has any right to expect from recitals of this species."

"I should not agree with you," replied Ferdinand, "if I was capable of explaining the mysterious connection between the portrait and the death of the two children in the same night, or the terror of Juliana at sight of the other portrait, and her death, consequently caused by it. I am, however, not the less obliged to you for the entire satisfaction you evince."

"But," resumed the young man, "what benefit would your imagination receive, if the connections of which you speak were known to you?"

"Very great benefit, without doubt," replied Ferdinand; "for imagination requires the completion of the objects it represents, as much as the judgment requires correctness and accuracy in its ideas."

The mistress of the house, not being partial to these metaphysical disputes, took part with Ferdinand: "We ladies," said she, "are always curious; therefore don't wonder that we complain when a story has no termination. It appears to me like seeing the last scene of Mozart's Don Juan without having witnessed the preceding ones; and *I* am sure no one would be the better satisfied, although the last scene should possess infinite merit."

The young man remained silent, perhaps less through conviction than politeness. Several persons were preparing to retire; and Ferdinand, who had vainly searched with all his eyes for the young lady with flaxen hair, was already at the door, when an elderly gentleman, whom he remembered to have seen in the music-room, asked him whether the friend concerning whom he had related the story was not called Count Meltheim?

"That is his name," answered Ferdinand a little dryly; "how did you guess it? - are you acquainted with his family?"

"You have advanced nothing but the simple truth," resumed the unknown. "Where is the count at this moment?"

"He is on his travels," replied Ferdinand. "But I am astonished –"

"Do you correspond with him?" demanded the unknown.

"I do," answered Ferdinand. "But I don't understand –"

"Well then," continued the old man, "tell him that Emily still continues to think of him, and that he must return as speedily as possible, if he takes any interest in a secret that very particularly concerns her family."

On this the old man stepped into his carriage, and had vanished from Ferdinand's sight ere he had recovered from his surprise. He looked around him in vain for some one who might inform him of the name of the unknown: every one was gone; and he was on the point of risking being considered indiscreet, by asking for information of the pastor who had so courteously treated him, when they fastened the door of the house, and he was compelled to return in sadness to his inn, and leave his researches till the morning.

The frightful scenes of the night preceding Ferdinand's departure from the *chateau* of his friend's father, had tended to weaken the remembrance of Emily; and the distraction which his journey so immediately after had produced, had not contributed to recall it with any force: but all at once the recollection of Emily darted across his mind with fresh vigour, aided by the recital of the previous evening and the old man's conversation: it presented itself even with greater vivacity and strength than at the period of its birth. Ferdinand now fancied that he could trace Emily in the pretty girl with flaxen hair. The more he reflected on her figure, her eyes, the sound of her voice, the grace with which she moved; the more striking the resemblance appeared to him. The piercing shriek that had escaped her, when he mentioned the old count's explication of the phantom's appearance; her sudden disappearance at the termination of the recital; her connection with Ferdinand's family, (for the young lady, in her history of Juliana, had recounted the fatal accident which actually befell Ferdinand's sister,) all gave a degree of certainty to his suppositions.

He passed the night in forming projects and plans, in resolving doubts and difficulties; and Ferdinand impatiently waited for the day which was to enlighten him. He went to the pastor's, whom he found in the midst of his quires of music; and by giving a natural turn to the conversation, he seized the opportunity of enquiring concerning the persons with whom he had passed the preceding evening.

He unfortunately, however, could not get satisfactory answers to his questions concerning the young lady with flaxen hair, and the mysterious old gentleman; for the pastor had been so absorbed in his music, that he had not paid attention to many persons who had visited him. and though Ferdinand in the most minute manner possible described their dress and other particulars, it was impossible to make the pastor comprehend the individuals whose names he was so anxious to learn. "It is unfortunate," said the pastor, "that my wife should be out; she would have given you all the information you desire. But according to your description, it strikes me the young person with flaxen hair must he Mademoiselle de Hainthal; -but-"

"Mademoiselle de Hainthal!" reiterated Ferdinand, somewhat abruptly.

"I think so," replied the clergyman. "Are you acquainted with the young lady?"

"I know her family," answered Ferdinand; "but from her features bearing so strong a resemblance to the family, I thought it might have been the young countess of Wartbourg, who was so much like her brother."

"That is very possible," said the pastor. "You knew then the unfortunate count Wartbourg?"

"Unfortunate!" exclaimed Ferdinand, greatly surprised.

"You don't then know any thing," continued the pastor, "of the deplorable event that has recently taken place at the chateau of Wartbourg? The young count, who had probably in his travels seen some beautifully laid-out gardens, was anxious to embellish the lovely country which surrounds his *chateau;* and as the ruins of an old tower seemed to be an obstacle to his plans, he ordered them to be pulled down. His gardener in vain represented to him, that seen from one of the wings of the *chateau* they presented, at the termination of a majestic and ancient avenue of linden trees, a magnificent coup d'oeil, and that they would also give a more romantic appearance to the new parts they were about to form. An old servant, grown grey in the service of his forefathers, supplicated him with tears in his eyes to spare the venerable remains of past ages. They even told him of an ancient tradition, preserved in the neighbourhood, which declared, that the existence of the house of Warthourg was by supernatural means linked with the preservation of that tower.

"The count, who was a well-informed man, paid no attention to these sayings; indeed they possibly made him the more firmly adhere to his resolution. The workmen were put to their task: the walls, which were constructed of huge masses of rock, for a long while resisted the united efforts of tools and gunpowder; the architect of this place appeared to have built it for eternity.

"At length perseverance and labour brought it down. A piece of the rock separating from the rest, precipitated itself into an opening which had been concealed for ages by rubbish and loose sticks, and fell into a deep cavern. An immense subterranean vault was discovered by the rays of the setting sun, supported by enormous pillars:- but ere they proceeded in their researches, they went to inform the young count of the discovery they had made.

"He came; and being curious to see this dark abode, descended into it with two servants. The first thing they discovered were chains covered with rust, which being fixed in the rock, plainly shewed the use formerly made of the cavern. On another side was a corpse, dressed in female attire of centuries past, which had surprisingly resisted the ravages of time: close to it was extended a human skeleton almost destroyed.

"The two servants related that the young count, on seeing the body, cried in an accent of extreme horror, 'Great God! it is she then whose portrait killed my intended wife.' Saying which, he fell senseless by the body. The shake which his fall occasioned reduced the skeleton to dust.

"They bore the count to his *chateau*, where the care of the physicians restored him to life; but he did not recover his senses. It is probable that this tragical event was caused by the confined and unwholesome air of the cavern. A very few days after, the count died in a state of total derangement.

"It is singular enough, that the termination of his life should coincide with the destruction of the ruined tower, and there no longer exists any male branch of that family. The deeds relative to the succession, ratified and sealed by the emperor Otho, are still amongst the archives of his house. Their contents have as yet only been transmitted verbally from father to son, as an hereditary secret, which will now, however, be made known. It is also true, that the affianced bride of the count was killed by the portrait's falling on her."

"I yesterday heard that fatal history recited by the lady with flaxen hair," replied Ferdinand.

"It is very possible that young person is the countess Emily," replied the pastor; "for she was the bosom-friend of the unfortunate bride."

"Does not then the countess Emily live at the castle of Wartbourg?" asked Ferdinand.

"Since her brother's death," answered the clergyman, "she has lived with a relation of her mother's at the *chateau* of Libinfelt, a short distance from hence. For as they yet know not with certainty to whom the castle of Wartbourg will belong, she prudently lives retired."

Ferdinand had learnt sufficient to make him abandon the projected journey to the capital. He thanked the pastor for the instructions he had given him, and was conducted to the *chateau* where Emily now resided.

It was still broad day when he arrived. The whole journey he was thinking of the amiable figure which he had recognised too late the preceding evening. He recalled to his idea her every word, the sound of her voice, her actions; and what his memory failed to represent, his imagination depicted with all the vivacity of youth, and all the fire of rekindled affection. He already addressed secret reproaches to Emily for not recognising him; as if he had himself remembered her; and in order to ascertain whether his features were entirely effaced from the recollection of her whom he adored, he caused himself to be announced as a stranger, who was anxious to see her on family matters.

While waiting impatiently in the room into which they had conducted him, he discovered among the portraits with which it was decorated, that of the young lady whose features had the over-night charmed him anew: he was contemplating it with rapture when the door opened and Emily entered. She instantly recognised Ferdinand; and in the sweetest accents accosted him as the friend of her youth.

Surprise rendered Ferdinand incapable of answering suitably to so gracious a reception: it was not the charming person with flaxen hair; it was not a figure corresponding with his imagination, which at this moment presented itself to his view.

But it was Emily, shining in every possible beauty, far beyond what Ferdinand had expected: he recollected notwithstanding each feature which had already charmed him, but now clothed in every perfection which nature bestows on her most favoured objects. Ferdinand was lost in thought for some moments: he dared not make mention of his love, and still less did he dare speak of the portrait, and the other wonders of the castle of Wartbourg. Emily spoke only of the happiness she had experienced in her earlier days, and slightly mentioned her brother's death. As the evening advanced, the young female with flaxen hair came in with the old stranger. Emily presented them both to Ferdinand, as the baron of Hainthal and his daughter Clotilde. They remembered instantly the stranger whom they had seen the preceding evening. Clotilde rallied him on his wish to be *incognito;* and he found himself on a sudden, by a short train of natural events, in the company of the person whom his mother intended for his wife; the object of his affection whom he had just discovered; and the interesting stranger who had promised him an explanation relative to the mysterious portraits.

Their society was soon augmented by the mistress of the *chateau* in whom Ferdinand recognised one of those who sat by his side the preceding evening. In consideration for Emily, they omitted all the subjects most interesting to Ferdinand; but after supper the baron drew nearer to him.

"I doubt not," said he to him, "that you are anxious to have some light thrown on events, of which, according to your recital last night, you were a spectator. I knew you from the first; and *I* knew also, that the story you related as of a friend, was your own history. *I* cannot, however, inform you of more than I know: but that will perhaps be sufficient to save Emily, for whom I feel the affection of a daughter, from chagrin and uneasiness; and from your recital of last evening, I perceive you take a lively interest concerning her."

"Preserve Emily from uneasiness," replied Ferdinand with warmth; "explain yourself: what is there I ought to do?"

"We cannot," answered the baron, "converse here with propriety; to morrow morning I will come and see you in your apartment."

Ferdinand asked him for an audience that night; but the baron was inflexible.

"It is not my wish," said he, "to work upon your imagination by any marvellous recital, but to converse with you on the very important concerns of two distinguished families. For which reason, I think the freshness of morning will be better suited to lessen the horror that my recital must cause you: therefore, if not inconvenient to you, I wish you to attend me at an early hour in the morning: I am fond of rising with the sun; and yet I have never found the time till mid-day too long for arranging my affairs," added he, smiling, and turning half round towards the rest of the party, as if speaking on indifferent topics.

Ferdinand passed a night of agitation, thinking of the conference he was to have with the baron; who was at his window at dawn of day. "You know," said the baron, "that I married the old count of Wartbourg's sister; which alliance was less the cause, than the consequence, of our intimate friendship. We reciprocally communicated our most secret thoughts, and the one never undertook any thing, without the other taking an equal interest with himself in his projects. The count had, however, one secret from me, of which I should never have come at the knowledge but for an accident.

"On a sudden, a report was spread abroad, that the phantom of the Nun's rock had been seen, which was the name given by the peasantry to the old ruined tower which you knew. Persons of sense only laughed at the report: I was anxious the following night to unmask this spectre, and I already anticipated my triumph: but to my no small surprise, the count endeavoured to dissuade me from the attempt; and the more I persisted, the more serious his arguments became; and at length he conjured me in the name of friendship to relinquish the design.

"His gravity of manner excited my attention; I asked him several questions; I even regarded his fears in the light of disease, and urged him to take suitable remedies: but he answered me with an air of chagrin, 'Brother, you know my sincerity towards you; but this is a secret sacred to my family. My son can alone be informed of it, and that only on my deathbed. Therefore ask me no more questions.'

"I held my peace; but I secretly collected all the traditions known amongst the peasantry. The most generally believed one was, that the phantom of the Nun's rock was seen when any one of the count's family were about to die; and in effect, in a few days after the count's youngest son expired. The count seemed to apprehend it: he gave the strictest possible charge to the nurse to take care of him; and under pretext of feeling indisposed himself, sent for two physicians to the castle: but these extreme precautions were precisely the cause of the child's death; for the nurse passing over the stones near the ruins, in her extreme care took the child in her arms to carry him, and her foot slipping, she fell, and in her fall wounded the child so much, that he expired on the spot. She said she fancied that she saw the child extended, bleeding in the midst of the stones; that her fright had made her fall with her face on the earth; and that when she came to herself, the child was absolutely lying weltering in his blood, precisely on the same spot where she had seen his ghost.

"I will not tire you with a relation of all the sayings uttered by on illiterate woman to explain the cause of the vision, for under similar accidents invention far outstrips reality. I could not expect to gain much more satisfactory information from the family records; for the principal documents were preserved in an iron chest, the key of which was never out of the possession of the owner of the castle. I however discovered, by the genealogical register and other similar papers that this family had never had collateral male branches; but further than this, my researches could not discover.

"At length, on my friend's death-bed I obtained some information, which, however, was far from being satisfactory. You remember that while the son was on his travels, the father was attacked by the complaint which carried him off so suddenly. The evening previous to his decease, he sent for me express, dismissed all those who were with him, and turning towards me, said: 'I am aware that my end is fast approaching, and I am the first of my family that has been carried off without communicating to his son the secret on which the safety of our house depends. Swear to me to reveal it only to my son, and I shall die contented.'

"In the names of friendship and honour, I promised what he exacted of me, and he thus began:

'The origin of my race, as you know, is not to be traced. Ditmar, the first of my ancestry mentioned in the written records, accompanied the emperor Otho to Italy. His history is also very obscure. He had an enemy called count Bruno, whose only son he killed in revenge, according to ancient tradition, and then kept the father confined till his death in that tower, whose ruins, situated in the Nun's rock, still defy the hand of time. That portrait which hangs alone in the state-chamber, is Ditmar's; and if the traditions of the family are to be believed, it was painted by the Dead. In fact, it is almost impossible to believe that any human being could have contemplated sufficiently long to paint the portrait, the outline of features so hideous. My forefathers have frequently tried to plaster over this redoubtable figure; but in the night, the colours came through the plaster, and re-appeared as distinctly as before; and often in the night, this Ditmar has been seen wandering abroad dressed in the garb represented in the picture; and by kissing the descendants of the family, has doomed them to death. Three of my children have received this fatal kiss. It is said, a monk imposed on him this penance in expiation of his crimes. But he cannot destroy all the children of his race: for so long as the ruins of the old tower shall remain, and whilst one stone shall remain on another, so long shall the count de Wartbourg's family exist; and so long shall the spirit of Ditmar wander on earth, and devote to death the branches of his house, without being able to annihilate the trunk. His race will never be extinct; and his punishment will only cease when the ruins of the tower are entirely dispersed. He brought up, with a truly paternal care, the daughter of his enemy, and wedded her to a rich and powerful knight; but notwithstanding this, the monk never remitted his penance. Ditmar, however, foreseeing that one day or other his race would perish, was certainly anxious ere then, to prepare for an event on which his deliverance depended;

and accordingly made a relative disposition of his hereditary property, in case of his family becoming extinct. The act which contained his will, was ratified by the emperor Otho: as yet it has not been opened, and nobody knows its contents. It is kept in the secret archives of our house.

"The speaking thus much was a great effort to my friend. He required a little rest, but was shortly after incapable of articulating a single word. I performed the commission with which he charged me to his son."

"And he did, notwithstanding –" replied Ferdinand.

"Even so," answered the baron: "but judge more favourably of your excellent friend. I have often seen him alone in the great state-chamber, with his eyes fixed on this horrible portrait: he would then go into the other rooms, where the portraits of his ancestors were ranged for several successive generations; and after contemplating them with visible internal emotion, would return to that of the founder of his house. Broken sentences, and frequent soliloquies, which I overheard by accident, did not leave me a shadow of doubt, but that he was the first of his race who had magnanimity of soul sufficient to resolve on liberating the spirit of Ditmar from its penance, and of sacrificing himself to release his house from the malediction that hung over it. Possibly he was strengthened in his resolutions by the grief he experienced for the death of his dearly beloved."

"Oh!" cried Ferdinand deeply affected, "how like my friend!"

"He had, however, in the ardour of his enthusiasm, forgotten to guard his sister's sensibility," said the baron.

"How so?" demanded Ferdinand.

"It is in consequence of this," answered the baron, "that I now address myself to you, and reveal to you the secret. I have told you that Ditmar demonstrated a paternal affection to the daughter of his enemy, had given her a handsome portion, and had married her to a valiant knight. Learn then, that this knight was Adalbert de Meltheim, from whom the counts of this name descended in a direct line."

"Is it possible?" exclaimed Ferdinand, "the author of my race!"

"The same," answered the baron; "and according to appearances, Ditmar designed that the family of Meltheim should succeed him on the extinction of his own. Haste, then, in order to establish your probable right to the –"

"Never - said Ferdinand" - so long as Emily –

"This is no more than I expected from you," replied the baron; "but remember, that in Ditmar's time the girls were not thought of in deeds of this kind. Your inconsiderate generosity would be prejudicial to Emily. For the next of kin who lay claim to the fief, do not probably possess very gallant ideas."

"As a relation, though only on the female side, *I* have taken the necessary measures; and I think it right you should be present at the castle of Wartbourg when the seals are broken, that you may be immediately recognised as the only immediate descendant of Adalbert, and that you may take instant possession of the inheritance."

"And Emily?" demanded Ferdinand.

"As for what is to be done for her," replied the baron, "I leave to you; and feel certain of her being provided for suitably, since her destiny will be in the hands of a man whose birth equals her own, who knows how to appreciate the rank in which she is placed, and who will evince his claims to merit and esteem."

"Have I a right, then," said Ferdinand, "to flatter myself with the hope that Emily will permit me to surrender her the property to which she is actually entitled?"

"Consult Emily on the subject," said the baron. - And here finished the conference.

Ferdinand, delighted, ran to Emily. She answered with the same frankness he had manifested; and they were neither of them slow to confess their mutual passion.

Several days passed in this amiable delirium. The inhabitants of the *chateau* participated in the joy of the young lovers; and Ferdinand at length wrote to his mother, to announce the choice he had made

They were occupied in preparations for removing to the castle of Wartbourg, when a letter arrived, which at once destroyed Ferdinand's happiness. His mother refused to consent to his marriage with Emily: her husband having, she said, on his death-bed, insisted on his wedding the baron of Hainthal's daughter, and that she should refuse her consent to any other marriage. He had discovered a family secret, which forced him peremptorily to press this point, on which depended his son's welfare, and the happiness of his family; she had given her promise, and was obliged to maintain it, although much afflicted at being compelled to act contrary to her son's inclinations.

In vain did Ferdinand conjure his mother to change her determination; he declared to her that he would be the last of his race, rather than renounce Emily. She was not displeased with his entreaties, but remained inflexible.

The baron plainly perceived, from Ferdinand's uneasiness and agitation, that his happiness had fled; and as he possessed his entire confidence, he soon became acquainted with the cause of his grief. He wrote in consequence to the countess Meltheim, and expressed his astonishment at the singular disposition the count had made on his death-bed but all he could obtain from her, was a promise to come to the castle of Wartbourg, to see the female whom she destined for her son, and the one whom he had himself chosen; and probably to elucidate by her arrival so singular and complicated an affair.

Spring was beginning to enliven all nature, when Ferdinand, accompanied by Emily, the baron, and his daughter, arrived at the castle of Wartbourg. The preparation which the principal cause of their journey required, occupied some days. Ferdinand and Emily consoled themselves in the hope that the countess of Meltheim's presence would remove every obstacle which opposed their love, and that at sight of the two lovers she would overcome her scruples.

A few days afterwards she arrived, embraced Emily in the most affectionate manner, and called her, her dear daughter, at the same time expressing her great regret that she could not really consider her such, being obliged to fulfil a promise made to her dying husband.

The baron at length persuaded her to reveal the motive for this singular determination: and after deliberating a short time, she thus expressed herself:

"The secret you are anxious I should reveal to you, concerns your family, Monsieur le Baron: consequently, if you release me from the necessity of longer silence, I am very willing to abandon my scruples. A fatal picture has, you know, robbed me of my daughter; and my husband, after this melancholy accident, determined on entirely removing this unfortunate portrait: he accordingly gave orders for it to be put in a heap of old furniture, where no one would think of looking for it; and in order to discover the best place to conceal it, he was present when it was taken there. In the removal, he perceived a piece of parchment behind the canvass which the fall had a little damaged: having removed it, he discovered it to be an old document, of a singular nature. The original of this portrait, (said the deed,) was called Bertha de Hainthal; she fixes her looks on her female descendants, in order that if any one of them should receive its death by this portrait, it may prove an expiatory sacrifice which will reconcile her to God. She will then see the families of Hainthal and Meltheim united by the bonds of love; and finding herself released, she will have cause to rejoice in the birth of her after-born descendants.

"This then is the motive which made my husband anxious to fulfil, by the projected marriage, the vows of Bertha; for the death of his daughter, caused by Bertha, had rendered her very name formidable to him. You see, therefore, I have the same reasons for adhering to the promise made my dying husband."

"Did not the count," demanded the baron, "allege any more positive reason for this command?"

"Nothing more, most assuredly," replied the countess.

"Well then," answered the baron, "in case the writing of which you speak should admit of an explanation wholly differing from, but equally clear with, the one attached thereto by the deceased, would you sooner follow the sense than the letter of the writing?"

"There is no doubt on that subject," answered the countess; "for no one is more anxious than myself to see that unfortunate promise set aside."

"Know then," said the baron, "that the corpse of that Bertha, who occasioned the death of your daughter, reposes here at Wartbourg and that, on this subject, as well as all the other mysteries of the castle, we shall have our doubts satisfied."

The baron would not at this time explain himself further; but said to the countess, that the documents contained in the archives of the castle would afford the necessary information; and recommended that Ferdinand should, with all possible dispatch, hasten every thing relative to the succession. Conformable to the baron's wish, it was requisite that, previous to any other research, the secret deeds contained in the archives should be opened. The law commissioners, and the next of kin who were present, who, most likely, promised themselves an ample compensation for their curiosity in the contents of the other parts of the records, were anxious to raise objections; but the baron represented to them, that the secrets of the family appertained to the unknown heir alone, and that consequently no one had a right to become acquainted with them, unless permitted by him.

These reasons produced the proper effect. They followed the baron into the immense vault in which were deposited the family records. They therein discovered an iron chest, which had not been opened for nearly a thousand years. A massive chain, which several times wound round it, was strongly fixed to the floor and to the wall; but the emperor's grand seal was a greater security for this sacred deposit, than all the chains and bolts which guarded it. It was instantly recognised and removed: the strong bolts yielded; and from the chest was taken the old parchment which had resisted the effects of time. This piece contained, as the baron expected, the disposition which confirmed the right of inheritance to the house of Meltheim, in case of the extinction of the house of Wartbourg: and Ferdinand, according to the baron's advice, having in readiness the deeds justifying and acknowledging him as the lawful heir to the house of Meltheim, the next of kin with regret permitted what they could not oppose; and he took possession of the inheritance. The baron having made him a signal, he immediately sealed the chest with his seal. He afterwards entertained the strangers in a splendid manner; and at night found himself in possession of his castle, with only his mother, Emily, the baron, and his daughter.

"It will be but just," said the baron, "to devote this night, which introduces a new name into this castle, to the memory of those who have hitherto possessed it. And we shall acquit ourselves most suitably in this duty, by reading in the council-chamber the documents which, without doubt, are destined to explain, as supplementary deeds, the will of Ditmar."

This arrangement was instantly adopted. The hearts of Emily and Ferdinand were divided between hope and fear; for they impatiently, yet doubtingly, awaited the *denouement* of Bertha's history, which, after so many successive generations, had in so incomprehensible a manner interfered with their attachment.

The chamber was lighted: Ferdinand opened the iron case; and the baron examined the old parchments.

"This," cried he, after having searched some short time, "will inform us." So saying, he drew from the chest some sheets of parchment. On the one which enveloped the rest was the portrait of a knight of an agreeable figure, and habited in the costume of the tenth century: and the inscription at the bottom called him Ditmar; but they could scarcely discover the slightest resemblance in it to the frightful portrait in the state-chamber. The baron offered to translate, in reading to them the document written in Latin, provided they would make allowances for the errors which were likely to arise from so hasty a translation. The curiosity of his auditors was so greatly excited, that they readily consented; and he then read as follows:

"I the undersigned Tutilon, monk of St. Gall, have, with the lord Ditmar's consent, written the following narrative: I have omitted nothing, nor written aught of my own accord.

"Being sent for to Metz, to carve in stone the image of the Virgin Mary; and that mother of our blessed Saviour having opened my eyes and directed my hands, so that I could contemplate her celestial countenance, and represent it on stone to be worshipped by true believers, the lord Ditmar discovered me, and engaged me to follow him to his castle, in order that I might execute his portrait for his descendants. I began painting it in the state-chamber of his castle; and on returning the following day to resume my task, I found that a strange hand had been at work, and had given the portrait quite a different countenance, which was horrible to look at, for it resembled one who had risen from the dead. I trembled with terror: however, I effaced these hideous features, and I painted anew the count Ditmar's figure, according to my recollection; but the following day I again discovered the nocturnal labour of the stranger hand. I was seized with still greater fear, but resolved to watch during the night; and I recommenced painting the knight's figure, such as it really was. At midnight I took a torch, and advancing softly into the chamber to examine the portrait, I perceived a spectre resembling the skeleton of a child; it held a pencil and was endeavouring to give Ditmar's image the hideous features of death.

"On my entering, the spectre slowly turned its head towards me, that I might see its frightful visage. My terror became extreme: I advanced no further, but retired to my room, where I remained in prayer till morning; for I was unwilling to interrupt the work executed in the dead of night. In the morning, discovering the same strange features in Ditmar's portrait as that of the two preceding mornings, I did not again risk effacing the work of the nightly painter ; but went in search of the knight, and related to him what I had seen. I shewed him the picture. He trembled with horror, and confessed his crimes to me, for which he required absolution. Having for three successive days invoked all the saints to my assistance, I imposed on him as a penance for the murder of his enemy, which he had avowed to me, to submit to the most rigid mortifications in a dungeon during the rest of his life. But I told him, that as he had murdered an innocent child, his spirit would never be at rest till it had witnessed the extermination of his race; for the Almighty would punish the death of that child by the death of the children of Ditmar, who, with the exception of one in each generation, would all be carried off in early life; and as for him, his spirit would wander during the night, resembling the portrait painted by the hand of the skeleton child; and that he would condemn to death, by a kiss, the children who were the sacrifices to his crimes, in the same manner as he had given one to his enemy's child before he killed it: and that, in fine, his race should not become extinct, so long as stone remained on stone in the tower where he had permitted his enemy to die of hunger. I then gave him absolution. He immediately made over his seigniory to his son; and married the daughter of his enemy, who had been brought up by him, to the brave knight Sir Adalbert. He bequeathed all his property, in case of his race becoming extinct, to this knight's descendants, and caused this will to be ratified by the emperor Otho. After having done so, he retired to a cave near the tower, where his corpse is interred; for he died like a pious recluse, and expiated his crimes by extreme penance. As soon as he was laid in his coffin, he resembled the portrait in the state-chamber; but during his life he was like the portrait depicted on this parchment, which I was able to paint without interruption, after having given him absolution: and by his command I have written and signed this document since his death; and I deposit it with the emperor's letters patent, in an iron chest, which I have caused to be sealed. I pray God speedily to deliver his soul, and to cause his body to rise from the dead to everlasting felicity!"

"He is delivered," cried Emily, greatly affected; "and his image will no longer spread terror around. But I confess that the sight of that figure, and even that of the frightful portrait itself, would never have led me to dream of such horrible crimes as the monk Tutilon relates. Certain I am, his enemy must have mortally wounded his happiness, or he undoubtedly would have been incapable of committing such frightful crimes."

"Possibly," said the baron, continuing his researches, "we shall discover some explanation on that point."

"We must also find some respecting Bertha," replied Ferdinand in a low tone, and casting a timid look on Emily and his mother.

"This night," answered the baron, "is consecrated to the memory of the dead; let us therefore forget our own concerns, since those of the past call our attention."

"Assuredly," exclaimed Emily, "the unfortunate person who secured these sheets in the chest, ardently looked forward to the hope of their coming to light; let us therefore delay it no longer."

The baron, after having examined several, read aloud these words:

"The confession of Ditmar." And he continued thus:- "Peace and health. When this sheet is drawn from the obscurity in which it is now buried, my soul will, I hope firmly in God and the saints, be at eternal rest and peace. But for your good I have ordered to be committed to paper the cause of my chastisement, in order that you may learn that vengeance belongs to God alone, and not to men; for the most just amongst them knows not how to judge: and again, that you may not in your heart condemn me, but rather that you may pity me; for my misery has nearly equalled my crimes; and my spirit would never have dreamt of evil, if man had not rent my heart."

"How justly," exclaimed Ferdinand, "has Emily's good sense divined thus much!"

The baron continued: "My name is Ditmar; they surnamed me 'The Rich', though I was then only a poor knight, and my only possession was a very small castle. When the emperor Otho departed for Italy, whither he was called by the beautiful Adelaide to receive her hand, I followed him and I gained the affection of the most charming woman in Pavia, whom I conducted as my intended spouse to the castle of my forefathers. Already the day appointed for the celebration of my nuptials was at hand: the emperor sent for me. His favourite, the count Bruno de Hainthal had seen Bertha —"

"Bertha!" exclaimed every one present. But the baron, without permitting them to interrupt him, continued his translation.

"One day, when the emperor had promised to grant him any recompense that he thought his services merited, he asked of him my intended bride. Otho was mute with astonishment; - but his imperial word was given. I presented myself before the emperor, who offered me riches, lands, honours, if I would but consent to yield Bertha to the count: but she was dearer to me than every worldly good. The emperor yielded to a torrent of anger: he carried off my intended bride by force, ordered my castle to be pulled down, and caused me to be thrown into prison.

"I cursed his power and my destiny. The amiable figure of Bertha, however, appeared to me in a dream; and I consoled myself during the day by the sweet illusions of the night. At length my keeper said to me: 'I pity you, Ditmar; you suffer in a prison for your fidelity, while Bertha abandons you. To-morrow she weds the count: accede then to the emperor's wish, ere it be too late ; and ask of him what you think fit, as a recompense for the loss of the faithless fair.' These words froze my heart. The following night, instead of the gracious image of Bertha, the frightful spirit of vengeance presented itself to me. The following morning I said to my keeper: 'Go and tell the emperor, I yield Bertha to his Bruno; but as a recompense, I demand this tower, and as much land as will be requisite to build me a new castle.' The emperor was satisfied; for he frequently repented his violent passions, but he could not alter what he had already decided. He therefore gave me the tower in which I had been confined, and all the lands around it for the space of four leagues. He also gave me more gold and silver than was sufficient to build a castle much more magnificent than the one he had caused to be pulled down. I took unto myself a wife, in order to perpetuate my race; but Bertha still reigned sole mistress of my heart. I also built myself a castle, from which I made a communication, by subterranean and secret passages, with my former prison the tower, and with the castle of Bruno, the residence of my mortal enemy. As soon as the edifice was completed, I entered the fortress by the secret passage, and appeared as the spirit of one of his ancestors before the bed of his son, the heir with which Bertha had presented him. The women who lay beside him were seized with fear: I leaned over the child, who was the precise image of its mother, and kissed its forehead; but - it was the kiss of death; it carried with it a secret poison.

"Bruno and Bertha acknowledged the vengeance of Heaven: they received it as a punishment for the wrongs they had occasioned me; and they devoted their first child to the service of God. As it was a girl, I spared it: but Bertha had no more children; and Bruno, irritated to find his race so nearly annihilated, repudiated his wife, as if he repented the injustice of which he had been guilty in taking her, and married another. The unfortunate Bertha took refuge in a monastery, and consecrated herself to Heaven: but her reason fled; and one night she quitted her retreat, came to the tower in which I had been confined in consequence of her perfidy, there bewailed her crime, and there grief terminated her existence; which circumstance gave rise to that tower being called the Nun's Rock. I heard, during the night, her sobs; and on going to the tower found Bertha extended motionless; the dews of night had seized her:-she was dead. I then resolved to avenge her loss. I placed her corpse in a deep vault beneath the tower; and having by means of my subterranean passage discovered all the count's movements, I attacked him when unguarded; and dragging him to the vault which contained his wife's corpse, I there abandoned him. The emperor, irritated against him for having divorced Bertha, gave me all his possessions, as a remuneration for the injustice I had heretofore experienced.

"I caused all the subterranean passages to be closed. I took under my care his daughter Hildegarde, and brought her up as my child: she loved the count Adalbert de Meltheim. But one night her mother's ghost appeared to her, and reminded her that she was consecrated to the Almighty: this vision, however, could not deter her from marrying Adalbert. The night of her marriage the phantom appeared again before her bed, and thus addressed her:

" 'Since you have infringed the vow I made, my spirit can never be at rest, till one of your female descendants receives its death from me.

"This discourse occasioned me to send for the venerable Tutilon, monk of St. Gall, who was very celebrated, in order that he might paint a portrait of Bertha, as she had painted herself in the monastery during her insanity; and I gave it to her daughter.

"Tutilon concealed behind that portrait a writing on parchment, the contents of which were as follows:

" 'I am Bertha; and I look at my daughters, to see whether one of them will not die for me, in expiation of my crimes, and thus reconcile me to God. Then shall I see the two families of Meltheim and Hainthal reunited by love, and in the birth of their descendants I shall enjoy happiness.' "

"This then," exclaimed Ferdinand, "is the fatal writing that is to separate me from Emily; but which, in fact, only unites me to her more firmly! and Bertha, delivered from her penance, blesses the alliance; for by my marriage with Emily, the descendants of Bertha of Ditmar will be reunited."

"Do you think," demanded the baron of the countess, "that this explanation can admit of the slightest doubt?"

The only answer the countess made, was by embracing Emily, and placing her hand in that of her son.

The joy was universal. Clotilde in particular had an air of extreme delight; and her father several times, in a jocular manner, scolded her for expressing her joy so vehemently. The following morning they removed the seals from the state-chamber, in order to contemplate the horrible portrait with somewhat less of sadness than heretofore; but they found that it had faded in a singular manner, and the colours, which formerly appeared so harsh, had blended and become softened.

Shortly after arrived the young man who was anxious to enter into an argument with Ferdinand on the explication of the mysteries relative to the portraits. Clotilde did not conceal that he was far from indifferent to her; and they discovered the joy she had evinced, in discovering the favourable turn Emily's attachment had taken, was not altogether disinterested, but occasioned by the prospect it afforded of happiness to herself. Her father, in fact, would never have approved her choice, had not the countess Meitheim removed all pretensions to Clotilde.

"But," asked Ferdinand of Clotilde's intended, "do you not forgive our having searched into certain mysteries which concerned us?"

"Completely," he answered; "but not less disinterestedly than formerly, when I maintained a contrary opinion. I ought now to confess to you, that I was present at the fatal accident which caused your sister's death, and that I then discovered the writing concealed behind the portrait. I naturally explained it as your father did afterwards; but I held my peace; for the consequences have brought to light what the discovery of that writing had caused me to apprehend for my love."

"Unsatisfactory explanations are bad," replied Ferdinand, laughing.

The happy issue of these discoveries spread universal joy amongst the inhabitants of the castle, which was in some degree heightened by the beauty of the season. The lovers were anxious to celebrate their marriage ere the fall of the leaf. And when next the primrose's return announced the approach of spring, Emily gave birth to a charming boy.

Ferdinand's mother, Clotilde and her husband, and all the friends of the family, among whom were the pastor who was so fond of music, and his pretty little wife, assembled at the fete given in honour of the christening. When the priest who was performing the ceremony asked what name he was to give the child that of Ditmar was uttered by every mouth, as if they had previously agreed on it. The christening over, Ferdinand, elate with joy, accompanied by his relations and guests, carried his son to the state chamber, before his forefather's portrait; but it was no longer perceptible; the colours, figure, - all had disappeared; not the slightest trace remained.

The Fated Hour

A heavy rain prevented the three friends from taking the morning's walk they had concerted: notwithstanding which, Amelia and Maria failed not to be at Florentina's house at the appointed hour. The latter had for some time past been silent, pensive, and absorbed in thought; and the anxiety of her friends made them very uneasy at the visible impression left on her mind by the violent tempest of the preceding night.

Florentina met her friends greatly agitated, and embraced them with more than usual tenderness.

"Fine weather for a walk!" cried Amelia: "how have you passed this dreadful night?"

"Not very well, you may easily imagine. My residence is in too lonely a situation."

"Fortunately," replied Maria, laughing, "it will not long be yours."

"That's true," answered Florentina, sighing deeply. "The count returns from his travels to-morrow, in the hope of soon conducting me to the altar."

"Merely in the hope'?" replied Maria: "the mysterious manner in which you uttered these words, leads me to apprehend you mean to frustrate those hopes?"

"I? But how frequently in this life does hope prove only an untimely flower?"

"My dear Florentina," said Maria, embracing her, "for some time past my sister and I have vainly attempted to account for your lost gaiety; and have been tormented with the idea, that possibly family reasons have induced you, contrary to your wishes, to consent to this marriage which is about to take place."

"Family reasons! Am I not then the last of our house; the only remaining one, whom the tombs of my ancestors have not as yet enclosed? And have I not for my Ernest that ardent affection which is natural to my time of life? Or do you think me capable of such duplicity, when I have so recently depicted to you, in the most glowing colours, the man of my heart's choice?"

"What then am I to believe?" inquired Maria. "Is it not a strange contradiction, that a young girl, handsome and witty, rich and of high rank, and who, independently of these advantages, will not by her marriage be estranged from her family, should approach the altar with trembling?"

Florentina, holding out her hand to the two sisters, said to them:

"How kind you are! I ought really to feel quite ashamed in not yet having placed entire confidence in your friendship, even on a subject which is to me, at this moment, incomprehensible. At this moment I am not equal to the task; but in the course of the day I hope to be sufficiently recovered. In the mean while let us talk on less interesting subjects."

The violent agitation of Florentina's mind was so evident at this moment that the two sisters willingly assented to her wishes. Thinking that the present occasion required trifling subjects of conversation, they endeavoured to joke with her on the terrors of the preceding night. However, Maria finished by saying, with rather a serious air,-

"I must confess, that more than once I have been tempted to think something extraordinary occurred. At first it appeared as if some one opened and shut the window of the room in which we slept, and then as if they approached my bed. I distinctly heard footsteps: an icy trembling seized me, and I covered my face over with the clothes."

"Alas!" exclaimed Amelia, "I cannot tell you how frequently I have heard similar noises. But as yet nothing have I seen."

"Most fervently do I hope," replied Florentina in an awful tone of voice, "that neither of you will ever, in this life, be subject to a proof of this nature!"

The deep sigh which accompanied these words, and the uneasy look she cast on the two sisters, produced evident emotions in them both.

"Possibly *you* have experienced such proof?" replied Amelia.

"Not precisely so: but - suspend your curiosity. This evening - if I am still alive - I mean to say - that this evening I shall be better able to communicate all to you."

Maria made a sign to Amelia, who instantly understood her sister; and thinking that Florentina wished to be alone, though evidently disturbed in her mind, they availed themselves of the first opportunity which her silence afforded. Her prayer book was lying open on the table, which, now perceiving for the first time, confirmed Maria in the idea she had conceived. In looking for her shawl she removed a handkerchief which covered this book, and saw that the part which had most probably occupied Florentina before their arrival was the Canticle on Death. The three friends separated, overcome and almost weeping, as if they were never to meet again.

Amelia and Maria awaited with the greatest impatience the hour of returning to Florentina. - They embraced her with redoubled satisfaction, for she seemed to them more gay than usual.

"My dear girls," said she to them, "pardon, I pray you, my abstraction of this morning. Depressed by having passed so bad a night, I though myself on the brink of the grave; and fancied it needful to make up my accounts in this world, and prepare for the next. I have made my will, and have placed it in the magistrate's hands: however, since I have taken a little repose this afternoon, I find myself so strong, and in such good spirits, that I feel as if I had escaped the danger which threatened me."

"But, my dear," replied Maria, in a mild yet affectionate tone of reproach, "how could one sleepless night fill your mind with such gloomy thoughts?"

"I agree with you on the folly of permitting it so to do; and had I encouraged sinister thoughts, that dreadful night would not have been the sole cause, for it found me in such a frame of mind that its influence was not at all necessary to add to my horrors. But no more of useless mystery. I must fulfill my promise, and clear up your doubts on many parts of my manner and conduct, which at present must appear to you inexplicable. Prepare yourselves for the strangest and most surprising events. - But the damp and cold evening air has penetrated this room, it will therefore be better to have a fire lighted, that the chill which my recital may produce be not increased by any exterior cause."

While they were lighting the fire, Maria and her sister expressed great joy at seeing such a happy change in Florentina's manner; and the latter could scarcely describe the satisfaction she felt, at having resolved to develop to them the secret which she had so long concealed. The three friends being alone, Florentina began as follows:-

"You were acquainted with my sister Seraphina, whom I had the misfortune to lose; but I alone can boast of possessing her confidence; which is the cause of my mentioning many things relative to her, before I begin the history I have promised, in which she is the principal personage.

"From her infancy, Seraphina was remarkable for several singularities. She was a year younger than myself; but frequently, while seated by her side I was amusing myself with the playthings common to our age, she would fix her eyes, by the half hour together, as if absorbed in thought: she seldom took any part in our infantine amusements. This disposition greatly chagrined our parents; for they attributed Seraphina's indifference to stupidity; and they were apprehensive this defect would necessarily prove an obstacle in the education requisite for the distinguished rank we held in society, my father being, next the prince, the first person in the country. They had already thought of procuring for her a canonry from some noble chapel, when things took an entirely different turn.

"Her preceptor, an aged man, to whose care they had confided her at a very early age, assured them, that in his life he had never met with so astonishing an intellect as Seraphina's. My father doubted the assertion: but an examination, which he caused to be made in his presence, convinced him that it was founded in truth.

"Nothing was then neglected to give Seraphina every possible accomplishment:- masters of different languages, of music, and of dancing, every day filled the house.

"But in a short time my father perceived that he was again mistaken: for Seraphina made so little progress in the study of the different languages, that the masters shrugged their shoulders; and the dancing-master pretended, that though her feet were extremely pretty, he could do nothing with them, as her head seldom took the trouble to guide them.

"By way of retaliation, she made such wonderful progress in music that she soon excelled her masters. She sang in a manner superior to that of the best opera-singers.

"My father acknowledged that his plans for the education of this extraordinary child were now as much too enlarged, as they were before too circumscribed; and that it would not do to keep too tight a hand over her, but let her follow the impulse of her own wishes.

This new arrangement afforded Seraphina the opportunity of more particularly studying the science of astronomy; which was one they had never thought of as needful for her. You can, my friends, form but a very indifferent idea of the avidity with which (if so I may express myself) she devoured those books which treated on celestial bodies; or what rapture the globes and telescopes occasioned her, when her father presented them to her on her thirteenth birth-day.

"But the progress made in this science in our days did not long satisfy Seraphina's curiosity. To my father's great grief, she was wrapped up in reveries of astrology; and more than once she was found in the morning occupied in studying books which treated on the influence of the stars, and which she had begun to peruse the preceding evening.

"My mother, being at the point of death, was anxious, I believe, to remonstrate with Seraphina on this whim; but her death was too sudden. My father thought that at this tender age Seraphina's whimsical fancy would wear off: however, time passed on, and he found that she still remained constant to a study she had cherished from her infancy.

"You cannot forget the general sensation her beauty produced at court: how much the fashionable versifiers of the day sang her graceful figure and beautiful flaxen locks; and how often they failed, when they attempted to describe the particular and indefinable character which distinguished her fine blue eyes. I must say, I have often embraced my sister, whom I loved with the greatest affection, merely to have the pleasure of getting nearer, if possible, to her soft angelic eyes, from which Seraphina's pale countenance borrowed almost all its sublimity.

"She received many extremely advantageous proposals of marriage, but declined them all. You know her predilection in favour of solitude, and that she never went out but to enjoy my society. She took no pleasure in dress; nay, she even avoided all occasions which required more than ordinary expense. Those who were not acquainted with the singularity of her character might have accused her of affectation.

"But a very extraordinary particularity, which I by chance discovered in her just as she attained her fifteenth year, created an impression of fear on my mind which will never be effaced.

"On my return from making a visit, I found Seraphina in my father's cabinet, near the window, with her eyes fixed and immovable. Accustomed from her earliest infancy to see her in this situation, without being perceived by her I pressed her to my bosom, without producing on her the least sensation of my presence. At this moment I looked towards the garden, and I there saw my father walking with this same Seraphina whom I held in my arms.

" 'In the name of God, my sister-' exclaimed I, equally cold with the statue before me; who now began to recover.

"At the same time my eye involuntarily returned towards the garden, where I had seen her; and there perceived my father alone, looking with uneasiness, as it appeared to me, for her, who, but an instant before, was with him. I endeavoured to conceal this event from my sister; but in the most affectionate tone she loaded me with questions to learn the cause of my agitation.

"I eluded them as well as I could; and asked her how long she had been in the closet. She answered me, smiling, that I ought to know best; as she came in after me; and that if she was not mistaken, she had before that been walking in the garden with my father.

"This ignorance of the situation in which she was but an instant before, did not astonish me on my sister's account, as she had often shewn proofs of this absence of mind. At that instant my father came in, exclaiming: 'Tell me, my dear Seraphina, how you so suddenly escaped from my sight, and came here? We were, as you know, conversing; and scarcely had you finished speaking, when, looking round, I found myself alone. I naturally thought that you had concealed yourself in the adjacent thicket; but in vain I looked there for you; and on coming into this room, here I find you.'

" 'It is really strange,' replied Seraphina; 'I know not myself how it has happened.'

"From that moment I felt convinced of what I had heard from several persons, but what my father always contradicted; which was, that while Seraphina was in the house, she had been seen elsewhere. I secretly reflected also on what my sister had repeatedly told me, that when a child (she was ignorant whether sleeping or awake), she had been transported to heaven, where she had played with angels; to which incident she attributed her disinclination to all infantine games.

"My father strenuously combated this idea, as well as the event to which I had been witness, of her sudden disappearance from the garden.

" 'Do not torment me any longer,' said he, 'with these phenomena, which appear complaisantly renewed every day, in order to gratify your eager imagination. It is true, that your sister's person and habits present many singularities; but all your idle talk will never persuade me that she holds any immediate intercourse with the world of spirits.'

"My father did not then know, that where there is any doubt of the future, the weak mind of man ought not to allow him to profane the word *never,* by uttering it.

"About a year and half afterwards, an event occurred which had power to shake even my father's determined manner of thinking to its very foundation. It was on a Sunday, that Seraphina and I wished at last to pay a visit which we had from time to time deferred: for notwithstanding my sister was very fond of being with me, she avoided even my society whenever she could not enjoy it but in the midst of a large assembly, where constraint destroyed all pleasure.

"To adorn herself for a party, was to her an anticipated torment; for she said, she only submitted to this trouble to please those whose frivolous and dissipated characters greatly offended her. On similar occasions she sometimes met with persons to whom she could not speak without shuddering, and whose presence made her ill for several days.

"The hour of assembling approached; she was anxious that I should go without her: my father doubting her, came into our room, and insisted on her changing her determination.

" 'I cannot permit you to infringe every duty.'

"He accordingly desired her to dress as quickly as possible, and accompany me.

"The waiting-maid was just gone out on an errand with which I had commissioned her. My sister took a light to fetch her clothes from a wardrobe in the upper story. She remained much longer absent than was requisite. At length she returned without a light: - I screamed with fright. My father asked her in an agitated manner, what had happened to her. In fact, she had scarcely been absent a quarter of an hour, and yet during that time her face had undergone a complete alteration; her habitual paleness had given place to a death-like hue; her ruby lips were turned blue.

"My arms involuntarily opened to embrace this sister whom I adored. I almost doubted my sight for I could get no answer from her; but for a long while she leaned against my bosom, mute and inanimate. The look, replete with infinite softness, which she gave my father and me, alone informed us, that during her continuance in this incomprehensible trance, she still belonged to the material world.

'I was seized with a sudden indisposition,' she at length said in a low voice; 'but I now find myself better.'

"She asked my father whether he still wished her to go into society. He thought, that after an occurrence of this nature her going out might be dangerous: but he would not dispense with my making the visit, although I endeavoured to persuade him that my attention might be needful to Seraphina. I left her with an aching heart.

"I had ordered the carriage to be sent for me at a very early hour: but the extreme anxiety I felt would not allow me to wait its arrival, and I returned home on foot. The servant could scarcely keep pace with me; such was my haste to return to Seraphina.

"On my arrival in her room, my impatience was far from being relieved. 'Where is she?' I quickly asked.

" 'Who mademoiselle?'

" 'Why, Seraphina.'

" 'Mademoiselle, Seraphina is in your father's closet.'

" 'Alone?'

" 'No with his Excellency.'

"I ran to the boudoir: the door, which was previously shut, at that instant opened, and my father with Seraphina came out: the latter was in tears. I remarked that my father had an air of chagrin and doubt which not even the storms of public life had ever produced in his countenance.

"He made us a sign full of gentleness, and Seraphina followed me into another room: but she first assured my father she would remember the promise he had exacted, and of which I was still ignorant."

"Seraphina appeared to me so tormented by the internal conflicts she endured, that I several times endeavoured, but in vain, to draw from her the mysterious event which had so recently thrown her into so alarming a situation. At last I overcame her scruples, and she answered me as follows:

" 'Your curiosity shall be satisfied, in part. I will develop some of the mystery to you; but only on one irrevocable condition.'

"I entreated her instantly to name the condition: and she thus continued:-

" 'Swear to me, that you will rest satisfied with what I shall disclose to you, and that you will never urge nor use that power which you possess over my heart, to obtain a knowledge of what I am obliged to conceal from you.'

"I swore it to her.

" 'Now, my dear Florentina, forgive me, if, for the first time in my life, I have a secret from you; and also for not being satisfied with your mere word for the promise I have exacted from you. My father, to whom I have confided every thing, has imposed these two obligations on me, and his last words were to that effect.'

"I begged her to come to the point.

" 'Words are inadequate to describe,' said she, 'the weight I felt my soul oppressed with when I went to get my clothes. I had no sooner closed the door of the room in which you and my father were, than I fancied I was about to be separated from life and all that constituted my happiness; and that I had many dreadful nights to linger through, ere I could arrive at a better and more peaceful abode. The air which I breathed on the staircase was not such as usually circulates around us; it oppressed my breathing, and caused large drops of icy perspiration to fall from my forehead. Certain it is, I was not alone on the staircase; but for a long while I dared not look around me.

" 'You know, my dear Florentina, with what earnestness I wished and prayed, but in vain, that my mother would appear to me after her death, if only for once. I fancied that on the stairs I heard my mother's spirit behind me. I was apprehensive it was come to punish me for the vows I had already made.'

" 'A strange thought, certainly!'

"'But how could I imagine that a mother, who was goodness itself, could be offended by the natural wishes of a tenderly beloved child, or have imputed them to indiscreet curiosity? It was no less foolish to think that she, who had been so long since enclosed in the tomb, should occupy herself in inflicting chastisement on me, for faults which were nearly obliterated from my recollection. I was so immediately convinced of the weakness of giving way to such ideas, that I summoned courage and turned my head.

" 'Although my affrighted survey could discover nothing, I again heard the footsteps following me, but more distinctly than before. At the door of the room I was about to enter, I felt my gown held. Overpowered by terror, I was unable to proceed, and fell on the threshold of the door.

" 'I lost no time, however, in reproaching myself for suffering terror so to overcome me; and recollected that there was nothing supernatural in this accident, for my gown had caught on the handle of an old piece of furniture which had been placed in the passage, to be taken out of the house the following day.

"'This discovery inspired me with fresh courage. I approached the wardrobe: but judge my consternation, when, preparing to open it, the two doors unclosed of themselves, without making the slightest noise; the lamp which I held in my hand was extinguished, and - as if I was standing before a looking-glass, - my exact image came out of the wardrobe: the light which it spread, illumined the great part of the room.

" 'I then heard these words: - Why tremble you at the sight of your own spirit, which appears to give you warning of your approaching dissolution, and to reveal to you the fate of your house?'

" 'The phantom then informed me of several future events. But when, after having deeply meditated on its prophetic words, I asked a question relative to you, the room became as dark as before, and the spirit had vanished. This, my dear, is all I am permitted to reveal.'

" 'Your approaching death!' cried I: - That thought had in an instant effaced all other.

"Smiling, she made me a sign in the affirmative; and gave me to understand, at the same time, that I ought to press her no further on this subject.' My father, added she, 'has promised to make you acquainted, in proper time, with all it concerns you to know.'

" 'At a proper time!' repeated I, in a plaintive voice; for it appeared to me, that since I had learned so much, it was high time that I should be made acquainted with the whole.

" 'The same evening I mentioned my wishes to my father: but he was inexorable. He fancied that possibly what had happened to Seraphina might have arisen from her disordered and overheated imagination. However, three days afterwards, my sister finding herself so ill as to be obliged to keep her bed, my father's doubts began to be shaken; and although the precise day of Seraphina's death had not been named to me, I could not avoid observing by her paleness, and the more than usually affectionate manner of embracing my father and me, that the time of our eternal separation was not far off.

" 'Will the clock soon strike nine?' asked Seraphina, while we were sitting near her bed in the evening.

"'Yes, soon,' replied my father.

"'Well then! Think of me, dear objects of my affection: - we shall meet again.' She pressed our hands; and the clock no sooner struck, than she fell back in her bed, never to rise more.

"My father has since related to me every particular as it happened; for at that time I was so much overcome that my senses had forsaken me.

"Seraphina's eyes were scarcely closed, when I returned to a life which then appeared to me insupportable. I was apprehensive that the state of stupefaction into which I was thrown by the dread of the loss that threatened me, had appeared to my sister a want of attachment. And from that time I have never thought of the melancholy scene without experiencing a violent shuddering.

"'You must be aware,' said my father to me (it was at the precise hour, and before the same chimney we are at this moment placed) – 'you must be aware, that the pretended vision should still be kept quite secret.' I was of his opinion; but could not help adding, 'What! Still, my father, though one part of the prediction has in so afflicting a manner been verified, you continue to call it a pretended vision?'

"'Yes, my child; you know not what a dangerous enemy to man is his own imagination. Seraphina will not be the last of its victims.'

"We were seated, as I before said, just as we now are; and I was about to name a motive which I had before omitted, when I perceived that his eyes were fixed in a disturbed manner on the door. I was ignorant of the cause, and could discover nothing extraordinary there: notwithstanding, however, an instant afterwards it opened of its own accord."

Here Florentina stopped, as if overcome anew by the remembrance of her terror. At the same moment Amelia rose from her seat uttering a loud scream.

Her sister and her friend inquired what ailed her. For a long while she made them no reply, and would not resume her seat on the chair, the back of which was towards the door. At length, however, she confessed (casting an inquiring and anxious look around her) that a hand, cold as ice, had touched her neck.

"This is truly the effect of imagination," said Maria, reseating herself. "It was my hand; for some time my arm has been resting on your chair; and when mention was made of the door opening of its own accord, I felt a wish to rest on some living object –"

"But à-propos, - And the door -?"

"Strange incident! I trembled with fear; and clinging to my father, asked him if he did not see a sort of splendid light, a something brilliant, penetrate the apartment.

"'Tis well!' answered he, in a low and tremulous voice, 'we have lost a being whom we cherished; and consequently, in some degree, our minds are disposed to exalted ideas and our imaginations may very easily be duped by the same illusions: besides, there is nothing very unnatural in a door opening of its own accord.'

"'It ought to be closely shut now,' replied I; without having the courage to do it.

"'Tis very easy to shut it,' said my father. But he rose in visible apprehension, walked a few paces, and then returned, adding, 'The door may remain open; for the room is too warm.

"It is impossible for me to describe, even by comparison, the singular light I had perceived and I do assure you, that if, instead of the light, I had seen my sister's spirit enter, I should have opened my arms to receive it; for it was only the mysterious and vague appearance of this strange vision which caused me so much fear.

"The servants coming in at this instant with supper, put an end to the conversation.

"Time could not efface the remembrance of Seraphina; but it wore off all recollection of the last apparition. My daily intercourse with you, my friends, since the loss of Seraphina, has been for me a fortunate circumstance, and has insensibly become an indispensable habit. I no longer thought deeply of the prediction relative to our house, uttered by the phantom to my sister; and in the arms of friendship gave myself up entirely to the innocent gaiety which youth inspires. The beauties of spring contributed to the restoration of my peace of mind. One evening, just as you had left me, I continued walking in the garden, as if intoxicated with the delicious vapours emitted from the flowers, and the magnificent spectacle which the serenity of the sky presented to my view.

"Absorbed entirely by the enjoyment of my existence, I did not notice that it was later than my usual hour for returning. And I know not why, but that evening no one appeared to think of me; for my father, whose solicitude for every thing concerning me was redoubled since my sister's death, and who knew I was in the garden, had not, as was his usual custom, sent me any garment to protect me from the chilling night air.

"While thus reflecting, I was seized with a violent feverish shivering which I could by no means attribute to the night air. My eyes accidentally fixed on the flowering shrubs; and the same brilliant light which I had seen at the door of the room on the day of Seraphina's burial, appeared to me to rest on these shrubs, and dart its rays towards me. The avenue in which I was happened to have been Seraphina's favourite walk.

"The recollection of this inspired me with courage, and I approached the shrubs in the hope of meeting my sister's shade beneath the trees. But my hopes being frustrated, I returned to the house with trembling steps. I there found many extraordinary circumstances: nobody had thought of supper, which I imagined would have been half over. All the servants were running about in confusion, and were hastening to pack up the clothes and furniture. "

" 'Who is going away?' I demanded.

" 'Why surely, mademoiselle!' exclaimed the steward, 'are you acquainted with his Excellency's wish to have us all?'

" 'Wherefore then?'

" 'This very night we are to set out for his Excellency's estate.'

" 'Why so?'

"They shrugged their shoulders. I ran into my father's cabinet, and there found him with his eyes fixed on the ground."

" 'Seraphina's second prophecy is also accomplished,' said he to me, 'though precisely the least likely thing possible. - I am in disgrace.'

"'' 'What! Did she predict this?'

" 'Yes, my child; but I concealed it from you. I resign myself to my fate, and leave others better to fill this perilous post. I am about to retire to my own estates, there to live for you, and to constitute the happiness of my vassals.'

"In spite of the violent emotions which were created by my father's misfortune, and the idea of separating from all the friends I loved, his apparent tranquillity produced a salutary effect on my mind. At midnight we set off. My father was so much master of himself under his change of condition, that by the time he arrived at his estate he was calm and serene.

"He found many things to arrange and improve; and his active turn of mind soon led him to find a train of pleasing occupations.

"In a short time, however, he was withdrawn from them by an illness which the physicians regarded as very serious. My father conformed to all they prescribed: he abstained from all occupation, though he entertained very little hope of any good resulting from it. 'Seraphina,' he said to me (entirely changing his former opinion), 'Seraphina has twice predicted true; and will a third time.'

"This conversation made me very miserable; for I understood from it that my father believed he should shortly die.

"In fact, he visibly declined, and was at length forced to keep his bed. He one evening sent for me; and after having dismissed his attendants, he, in a feeble voice, and with frequent interruptions, thus addressed me:-

"'Experience has cured me of incredulity; When the clock strikes nine, according to Seraphina's prediction, I shall be no more. For this reason, my dear child, I am anxious to address a few words of advice to you. If possible, remain in your present state; never marry. Destiny appears to have conspired against our race. - But no more of this. - To proceed: if ever you seriously think of marrying, do not, I beseech you, neglect to read this paper; but my express desire is, that you do not open it beforehand, as in that case its contents would cause you unnecessary misery.'

"Saying these words, which with sobbing I listened to, he drew from under his pillow a scaled paper, which he gave me. The moment was not favourable for reflecting on the importance of the condition which he imposed on me. The clock, which announced the *fated hour,* at which my father, resting on my shoulder, drew his last gasp, deprived me of my senses.

"The day of his interment was also marked by the brilliant and extraordinary light of which I have before made mention.

"You know, that shortly after this melancholy loss I returned to the capital, in hopes of finding consolation in your beloved society. You also know, that youth seconded your efforts to render existence desirable, and that by degrees I felt a relish for life. Neither are you ignorant that the result of this intercourse was an attachment between the count Ernest and me, which rendered my father's exhortations abortive. The count loved me, and I returned his affection, and nothing more was wanting to make me think that I ought not to lead a life of celibacy: besides, my father had only made this request conditionally.

"My marriage appeared certain; and I did not hesitate to open the mysterious paper. There it is, I will read it to you:-

"'Seraphina has undoubtedly already told you, that when she endeavoured to question the phantom concerning your destiny, it suddenly disappeared. The incomprehensible being seen by your sister had made mention of you, and its afflicting decree was, that three days before that fixed on for your marriage, you would die at the same *ninth* hour which has been so fatal to us. Your sister recovering a little from her first alarm, asked it, if you could not escape this dreadful mandate by remaining single.

" 'Unhappily, Seraphina did not receive any answer: but I feel assured, that by marrying you will die. For this reason I entreat you to remain single: I add, however - if it accords with your inclinations; as I do not feel confident that even this will ensure you from the effect of the prediction.

" 'In order, my dear child, to save you from all this premature uneasiness, I have avoided this communication till the hour of danger: reflect, therefore, seriously on what you ought to do.

" 'My spirit, when you read these lines, shall hover over and bless you, whatever way you decide.' "

Florentina folded up the paper again in silence; and, after a pause which her two friends sensibly felt, added:-

"Possibly, my dear friends, this has caused the change in me which you have sometimes condemned. But tell me whether, situated as I am, you would not become troubled, and almost annihilated, by the prediction which announced your death on the very eve of your happiness?

"Here my recital ends. To-morrow the count returns from his travels. The ardour of his affection had induced him to fix on the third day after his arrival for the celebration of our marriage."

"Then 'tis this very day!" exclaimed Amelia and Maria at the same moment; paleness and inquietude depicted on every feature when their eyes glanced to a clock on the point of striking nine.

"Yes, this is indeed the decisive day," replied Florentina, with a grave yet serene air. "The morning has been to me a frightful one; but at this moment I find myself composed, my health is excellent, and gives me a confidence that death would with difficulty overcome me to-day. Besides, a secret but lively presentiment tells me that this very evening the wish I have so long formed will be accomplished. My beloved sister will appear to me, and will defeat the prediction concerning me.

"Dear Seraphina! You were so suddenly, so cruelly snatched from me! Where are you, that I may return, with tenfold interest, the love that I have not the power of proving towards you?"

The two sisters, transfixed with horror, had their eyes riveted on the clock, which struck the fated hour.

"You are welcome!" cried Florentina, seeing the fire in the chimney, to which they had paid no attention, suddenly extinguished. She then rose from her chair; and with open arms walked towards the door which Maria and Amelia anxiously regarded, whilst sighs escaped them both; and at which entered the figure of Seraphina, illumined by the moon's rays. Florentina folded her sister in her arms. – "I am thine for ever!"

These words, pronounced in a soft and melancholy tone of voice, struck Amelia and Maria's ears; but they knew not whether they were uttered by Florentina or the phantom, or whether by both the sisters together.

Almost at the same moment the servants came in, alarmed, to learn what had happened. They had heard a noise as if all the glasses and porcelain in the house were breaking. They found their mistress extended at the door, but not the slightest trace of the apparition remained.

Every means of restoring Florentina to life were used, but in vain. The physicians attributed her death to a ruptured blood-vessel. Maria and Amelia will carry the remembrance of this heart-rending scene to their graves.

The Death Head

THE beauty of the evening which succeeded to a very sultry day tempted colonel Kielholm to sit, surrounded by his little family, on the stone bench placed before the door of the noble mansion he had recently purchased. In order to become acquainted by degrees with his new tenants, he took pleasure in questioning on their occupations and conditions the greater part of those who passed by; he alleviated their little sufferings by his advice as well as by his bounty. His family enjoyed particular pleasure in seeing the little inn situated in front of the chateau, which, instead of presenting a disgusting object, as when the late owner lived there, became each succeeding day better and more orderly. Their pleasure was heightened from the circumstance that the new landlord, who had been many years a servant in the family, was loud in praises of its amended condition, and delighted himself in his new calling, with the idea of the happy prospects it held forth to himself, his wife, and children.

Formerly, though the road was greatly frequented, nobody ventured to pass a night at this inn; but now each day there was a succession of travellers; carriages were constantly seen at the door or in the court-yard; and the air of general satisfaction of each party as they proceeded on their route, incontestably proved to the landlord, (who always, hat in hand, was at the door of their carriages as they drove off,) that his efforts to give the various travellers satisfaction were completely successful.

A moving scene of this nature had just disappeared, which furnished conversation for the moment, when a whimsical equipage, which arrived from another quarter, attracted the attention of the colonel and his family. A long carriage, loaded with trunks and all sorts of luggage, and drawn by two horses, whose form and colour presented the most grotesque contrast imaginable, but which in point of meagreness were an excellent match, was succeeded by a second long and large vehicle, which they had, most probably at the expense of the adjacent forest, converted into a travelling thicket. The four steeds which drew it, did not in any respect make a better appearance than the two preceding.

But the colonel and his family were still more struck by the individuals who filled this second carriage: it was a strange medley of children and grown persons, closely wedged together; but not one of their countenances bore the slightest mark of similarity of ideas. Discontent, aversion, and hatred, were legible in the face of each of these sun-burnt strangers. It was not a family, but a collection of individuals which fear or necessity kept together without uniting.

The colonel's penetrating eye led him to discover thus much, though the distance was considerable. He at length saw descend from the back part of the carriage a man of better appearance than the others. At something which he said, the whole troop turned their eyes towards the inn; they assumed an air of greater content, and appeared a little better satisfied.

The first carriage had already stopped at the door of the inn, while the second was passing the *chateau;* and the extremely humble salutations from the passengers in the latter, seemed to claim the goodwill of the colonel and his family.

The second carriage had scarcely stopped, ere the troop were out of it, each appearing anxious to quit those next to whom they had been sitting with all possible speed. The spruce and agile manner in which they leapt out of the vehicle, left no doubt on the mind what their profession was, they could be none other than rope-dancers.

The colonel remarked, that notwithstanding the humble salutations they had made, he did not think they would exhibit in these parts; but according to appearances they would proceed to the capital with all possible dispatch; as it was hardly to be expected that they would be delayed a single day, by the very trivial profit to he expected from exhibiting in a mere country village.

"We have," said he, "seen the worst side of these gentry, without the probability of ascertaining whether they have any thing to recommend them to our notice."

His wife was on the point of expressing her dislike to all those tricks which endanger the neck, when the person whom they had observed as being superior to the rest, advanced towards them, and after making bow, asked permission to remain there a few days. The colonel was unable to refuse this request, as he shewed him a passport properly signed.

"I beg you," replied the colonel, "to declare most positively to company, that every equivocal action is punished in my villages; as anxious to avoid all possibility of quarrels."

"Do not in the least alarm yourself, Monsieur; an extremely severe discipline is kept up in my troop, which has in some respects the efficiency of a secret police among ourselves: all can answer for one, and one can answer for all. Each is bound to communicate any misconduct, on the part of another, to me and is always rewarded for such communication; but on the contrary, if he omits so to do, he is severely punished."

The colonel's lady could not conceal her aversion to such a barbaric regulation; which the stranger perceiving, shrugged his shoulders.

"We must all accommodate our ideas to our condition. I have found that if persons of this stamp are not so treated, there is no possibility of governing them. And you may the more confidently rely on my vigilance as I had the happiness of being born in this place, and in consequence feel a double obligation: first, to the place of my birth; secondly, to worship."

"Were you born here?" demanded the colonel's wife with surprise.

"Yes, my lady; my father was Schurster the schoolmaster, who lately died. But I call myself Calzolaro, finding that my profession succeeds better under an Italian than a German name."

This explanation redoubled the interest the colonel and his lady already felt for this man, who appeared to have received a tolerable education. They knew that the schoolmaster, whose profession had been pretty lucrative, owing to the numerous population of the village, had died worth some considerable property; but that he had named a distant female relation as his sole heiress, leaving his only son an extremely scanty pittance.

"My father," continued Calzolaro, "did not behave to me as he ought and I cannot but think I should be justified in availing myself of some important informalities in his will, and endeavouring to set it aside which is my present intention. But excuse, I pray you, my having tired your patience with relations to which the conversation has involuntarily given rise. I have still one more request to make: Permit me to return my best thanks for your gracious condescension, and to show you some of the exercises for which my troop is famous."

The colonel acceded to Calzolaro's request, and a day was fixed for the performance.

Calzolaro went that very evening to the village pastor, and communicated to him his intentions relative to his father's will. The worthy minister condemned such procedure, and endeavoured to convince Calzolaro that his father's anger was just. "Picture to yourself, young man," said he, "a father who has grown old in an honest profession, and who rejoices in having a son to whom he can leave it: added to which, this son has great talents, a good understanding, and is well-disposed. It was natural that the father should use every possible exertion to obtain for this son his own situation at his death. The son is in truth nominated to succeed him. The father, thinking himself secure from misfortune, feels quite happy. It was at this period that the son, enticed by hair-brained companions, gave up a certain and respectable, though not very brilliant provision. My dear Schurster, if, when shaking off the salutary yoke, and quitting your venerable father, to ramble over the world, you could lightly forget the misery it would occasion him, you ought at least in the present instance to behave differently; or, in plain terms, I shall say you are a good-for-nothing fellow. Did not your father, even after this, do all he could to reclaim you? but you were deaf to his remonstrances."

"Because the connection which I had formed imposed obligations on me, from which I could not free myself, as from a garment of which one is tired. For had I then been my own master, as I now am –"

"Here let us stop, if you please: I have only one request to make of you. You ought, from respect to your father's memory, not to dispute his will."

This conversation and the venerable air of the pastor had a little shaken Calzolaro's resolutions: but the next day they returned with double force; for he heard several persons say, that shortly before his death, his father was heard to speak of him with great bitterness.

This discourse rendered him so indignant, that he would not even accede to a proposal of accommodation with the heiress, made to him by the pastor.

The colonel tried equally, but without success, to become a mediator, and at length determined to let the matter take its course.

He however assisted at the rehearsals made by the troop; and took so much pleasure in the performances prepared for the amusement of him and his family by Calzolaro, that he engaged him to act again, and invited several of his neighbours to witness them.

Calzolaro said to him on this occasion: "You have as yet seen very trifling proofs of our abilities. But do not fancy that I am an idle spectator and merely stand by to criticise:- I, as well as each individual of troop, have a sphere of action; and I reserve myself to give you, before take our leave, some entertaining experiments in electricity and magnetism."

The colonel then told him, that he had recently seen in the capita man who exhibited experiments of that sort, which had greatly delight him; and above all, he had been singularly astonished by his powers ventriloquism.

"It is precisely in that particular point," replied Calzolaro, "that I think myself equal to any one, be they whom they may."

"I am very glad of it," answered the colonel. "But what would produce the most astonishing effect on those who have never heard a ventriloquist, would be a dialogue between the actor and a death's head:- the man of whom I made mention gave us one."

"If you command it, I can undertake it."

"Delightful!" exclaimed the colonel. And Calzolaro having given some unequivocal proofs of his powers as a ventriloquist, the colonel added: "The horror of the scene must be augmented by every possible means: for instance, we must hang the room with black; the lights must be extinguished; we must fix on midnight. It will be a species of phantasmagoria dessert after supper; an unexpected spectacle. We must contrive to throw the audience into a cold perspiration, in order that when the explanation takes place they may have ample reason to laugh at their fears. For if all succeeds no one will be exempt from a certain degree of terror."

Calzolaro entered into the project, and promised that nothing should be neglected to make it successful. They unfurnished a closet, and hung it with black.

The colonel's wife was the only one admitted to their confidence, as they could rely on her discretion. Her husband had even a little altercation on the subject with her. She wished, that for the ventriloquist scene they should use the model of a head in plaster, which her son used to draw from; whereas the colonel maintained that they must have a real skull "Otherwise," said he, "the spectators' illusion will speedily be at an end but after they have heard the death's head speak, we will cause it to be handed round, in order to convince them that it is in truth but a skull."

"And where can we procure this skull?" asked the colonel's wife.

"The sexton will undertake to provide us with it."

"And whose corpse will you thus disturb, for a frivolous amusement?"

"How sentimental you are!" replied Kielholm, who did not consider the subject in so serious a light: "We may easily see you are not accustomed to the field of battle, where no further respect is paid to the repose of the dead, than suits the convenience of the labourer in the fields where they are buried."

"God preserve me from such a spectacle!" exclaimed the colonel's lady in quitting them, when she perceived her husband was insensible to her representations.

According to the orders which he received, the sexton one night brought a skull in good preservation.

The morning of the day destined for the representation, Calzolaro went into the adjacent forest to rehearse the dialogue which he was to have with the death's head. He considered in what way to place the head, so as to avoid all suspicion of the answers given by it being uttered by a person concealed. In the mean while the pastor arrived at the spot from a neighbouring hamlet, where he had been called to attend a dying person: and believing that the interposition of Providence was visible in this accidental meeting, the good man stopped, in order once again to exhort Calzolaro to agree to an accommodation with the heiress.

"I yesterday," said he, "received a letter from her, in which she declares that, rather than any disrespect should be paid to your father's last will and testament, she will give up to you half the inheritance to which she is thereby entitled. Ought you not to prefer this to a process at law, the issue of which is doubtful, and which at all events will never do you credit?"

Calzolaro persisted in declaring that the law should decide between him and the testator. - The poor young man was not in a state to see in a proper point of view his father's conduct towards him. - The pastor, finding all his representations and entreaties fruitless, left him. Calzolaro proceeded slowly to the inn, to assign to each of his band their particular part. He told them that he should not be with them; but notwithstanding he should have an eye over their conduct. He was not willing to appear as the manager of these mountebanks, to the party assembled at the colonel's, thinking that if he appeared for the first time in the midnight scene, as an entire stranger, it would add still more to the marvellous.

The tumblers' tricks and rope-dancing were performed to admiration. And those of the spectators whose constant residence in the country prevented their having witnessed similar feats, were the most inclined to admire and praise the agility of the troop. The little children in particular were applauded. The compassion excited by their unhappy destiny, mingled with the approbation bestowed on them; and the ladies were subject of envy, in giving birth to the satisfaction depicted in the countenances of these little wretches by their liberal donations.

The agility of the troop formed the subject of general conversation that whole afternoon. They were even speaking in their praise after supper, -when the master of the house said to the company assembled:

"I am rejoiced, my dear friends, to see the pleasure you have received from the little spectacle that I have been enabled to give you. My joy is so much the greater, since I find you doubting the possibility of things which are very natural; for I have it in my power to submit for your examination something of a very incomprehensible nature. At this very moment I have in my house a person who entertains a most singular intercourse with the world of spirits, and who can compel the dead to answer his questions"

"O!" exclaimed a lady smiling, "don't terrify us."

"You jest *now,*" replied the colonel; "but I venture to affirm your mirth will be a little changed when the scene takes place."

"I accept the challenge," answered the incredulous fair one. All the party was of her opinion, and declared themselves so openly and so loudly against the truth of these terrific scenes, that the colonel began to be really apprehensive for the effects likely to be produced by those he had prepared. He would have even relinquished his project, if his guests, one and all, had not entreated him to the contrary. They even went further: they besought him not long to delay the wonderful things he promised. But the colonel, keeping his own counsel, feigned ignorance that they were laughing at him; find with a grave air declared that the experiment could not take place till midnight.

The clock at length struck twelve. The colonel gave his servants orders to place chairs facing the door of a closet which had been hitherto kept shut: he invited the company to sit down, and gave orders for all the lights to be put out. While these preparations were making, he thus addressed the company:

"I entreat you, my friends, to abstain from all idle curiosity." The grave and solemn tone in which he uttered these words made a deep impression on the party, whose incredulity was not a little lessened by the striking of the clock, and the putting out the lights one after the other. Presently they heard from the closet facing them the hoarse and singular sounds by which it is pretended spirits are conjured up; and which were interrupted at intervals by loud strokes of a hammer. All on a sudden the door of the closet opened: and as by slow degrees the cloud of incense which filled it evaporated, they gradually discovered the black trappings with which it was hung, and an altar in the middle also hung with black drapery. On this altar was placed a skull, which cast its terrifying regards on all the company present.

Meanwhile the spectators' breathing became more audible and difficult, and their embarrassment increased in proportion as the vapour gave place to a brilliant light issuing from an alabaster lamp suspended from the ceiling. Many of them indeed turned their heads away in alarm on hearing a noise behind them; which, however, they discovered simply proceeded from some of the servants, whom the colonel had given permission to be present during the exhibition, at a respectful distance.

After a moment of profound silence, Calzolaro entered. A long beard had so effectually altered his youthful appearance, that though several of the spectators had previously seen him, they could not possibly recognise him under this disguise. And his Oriental costume added so much to the deceit, that his entrance had an excellent effect.

In order that his art should impose the more, the colonel recommended to him a degree of haughtiness in addressing the company; and that he should not salute them according to any prescribed forms of politeness, but to announce himself in terms foreign from all ordinary modes of conversation. They both agreed that a mysterious jargon would best answer their purpose.

In consequence of such determination, Calzolaro, assuming a deep sepulchral tone, thus began:- "After our present state of existence, we are swallowed up in the obscure abyss which we call death, in order that we may become incorporated in an entirely new and peaceful state. It is in order to emancipate the soul from this state, that the sublime arts are exercised; and to create among fools and weak persons the idea of its being impossible! The wise and learned pity them for their ignorance, in not knowing what is possible and impossible, true or false, light or dark; because they do not know and cannot comprehend the exalted spirits, who, from the silence of the vault and the grave, from the mouldering bones of the dead, speak to the living in a voice no less formidable than true. As to you, who are now here assembled, listen to a word of advice: avoid provoking by any indiscreet question the vengeance of the spirit, who at my command will be invisibly stationed beneath this human skull. Endeavour to moderate your fear: listen to every thing with calmness and submission; for I take under my especial care all those who are obedient, and only leave the guilty as a prey to the destruction they merit."

The colonel remarked with secret satisfaction the impression produced on the company, hitherto so incredulous, by this pompous harangue.

"Every thing succeeds better than I could have hoped," said he, in an undertone to his wife, who was not at all amused by the performance, and who was only present to please her husband.

Meanwhile Calzolaro continued: "Look on this pitiful and neglected head: my magic art has removed the bolts of the tomb to which it was consigned, and in which reposes a long line of princes. The owner of it is now actually there, rendering up to the spirits an exact account of the life he had led. Don't be alarmed, even though it should burst forth in terrible menaces against you: and against me his impotency will be manifest, as, spite of his former grandeur, he cannot resist the power I have over him, provided no culpable precipitation on your part interrupt the solemnity of my questions."

He then opened a door of the closet hitherto concealed from the company, brought a chafing dish filled with red-hot coals, threw thereon some Incense, and walked three times round the altar, pronouncing at each circle a spell. He then drew from its scabbard a sword which hung in his girdle, plunged it in the smoke issuing from the incense, and making frightful contortions of his face and limbs, pretended to endeavour to cleave the head, which, however, he did not touch. At last he took the head up on the point of his sword, held it up in the air before him, and advanced towards the spectators a little moved.

"Who art thou, miserable dust, that I hold at the point of my sword?" demanded Calzolaro with a confident air and a firm voice. - But scarcely had he uttered this question, then he turned pale; his arm trembled; his knees shook; his haggard eyes, which were fixed on the head, were horror-struck: he had hardly strength sufficient to place the head and the sword on the altar, ere he suddenly fell on the floor with every symptom of extreme terror.

The spectators, frightened out of their wits, looked at the master of the house, who in his turn looked at them: No one seemed to know whether this was to be considered part of the scene nor whether it was possible to explain it. The curiosity of the audience was raised to its utmost pitch: they waited still a considerable time, but no explanation took place. At length Calzolaro, half-raising himself, asked if his father's shadow had disappeared.

Stupefaction succeeded astonishment. The Colonel was anxious to know whether he was still attempting to impose on the company by a pretended dialogue with the death's head?

Calzolaro answered that he would do anything, and that he would willingly submit to any punishment they chose to inflict on him for his frightful crime: but he entreated they would instantly carry back the head to its place of repose.

His countenance had undergone a complete change, and only resumed its wonted appearance on the colonel's wife acquiescing in his wish: she ordered the head to be instantly conveyed to the churchyard, and to be replaced in the grave.

During this unexpected denouement, every eye was turned on Calzolaro; he, who not long ago was talking with so much emphasis and in such a lofty strain, could now scarcely draw his breath; and from time to time threw supplicating looks on the spectators, as if entreating them to wait patiently till he had recovered strength sufficient to continue his performance.

The colonel informed them in the meanwhile of the species of jest that he had projected to play on them, and for the failure of which he could not at that moment account. At last Calzolaro, with an abashed air, spoke as follows:-

"The spectacle which I designed to have given, has terminated in a terrible manner for me. But, happily for the honourable company present, I perceive they did not see the frightful apparition which caused me a temporary privation of my reason. Scarcely had I raised the death's head on the point of my sword, and had begun to address it, than it appeared to me in my father's features; and whether my ears deceived me or not, I am ignorant; neither do I know how I was restored to my senses; but I heard it say, 'Tremble, parricide, whom nothing can convert, and who wilt not turn to the path thou hast abandoned!' "

The very recollection produced such horror on Calzolaro's mind as to stop his respiration and prevent his proceeding. The colonel briefly explained to the spectators what appeared to them mysterious in his words, and then said to the penitent juggler:

"Since your imagination has played you so strange a trick, I exhort you in future to avoid all similar accidents, and to accept the arrangement proposed to you by the person whom your father has named as his heir."

"No, monsieur," answered he, "no agreement, no bargain; else I shall only half fulfil my duty. Every thing shall belong to this heiress, and the law-suit shall be abandoned."

He at the same time declared that he was weary of the mode of life he had adopted, and that every wish of his father's should be fulfilled.

The colonel told him that such a resolution compensated for what had failed in the evening's amusement.

The company, however, did not cease making numberless inquiries of Calzolaro, many of which were very ludicrous. They were anxious to know, among other things, whether the head which had appeared to him, resembled that of a corpse or a living being.

"It most probably belongs to a corpse," he replied. "I was so thunderstruck with the horrible effect of it, that I cannot remember minutiae. Imagine an only son, with the point of a sword which he holds in his hand, piercing his father's skull! The bare idea is sufficient to deprive one of one's senses."

"I did not believe," answered the colonel, after having for some time considered Calzolaro, "that the conscience of a man, who like you has rambled the world over, could still be so much overcome by the powers of imagination."

"What! monsieur, do you still doubt the reality of the apparition, though I am ready to attest it by the most sacred oaths?"

"Your assertion contradicts itself. We have also our eyes to see what really exists; and nobody, excepting yourself, saw any other than a simple skull."

"That is what I cannot explain: but this I can add, that I am firmly persuaded, although even now I cannot account for my so thinking, that as sure as I exist, that head is actually and truly the head of my father: I am ready to attest it by my most solemn oath."

"To prevent your perjuring yourself, they shall instantly go to the sexton, and learn the truth."

Saying this, the colonel went out to give the necessary orders. He returned an instant afterwards, saying:-

"Here is another strange phenomenon. The sexton is in this house, but is not able to answer my questions. Anxious to enjoy the spectacle I was giving my friends, he mixed with some of my servants, who, possessing the same degree of curiosity, had softly opened the door through which the chaffing-dish was conveyed. But at the moment of the conjurer falling on the floor, the same insensibility overcame the sexton; who even now has not recovered his reason, although they have used every possible method to restore him."

One of the party said, that, being subject to fainting himself, he constantly carried about him a liquor, the effect of which was wonderful in such cases, and that he would go and try it now on the sexton. They all followed him: but this did not succeed better than the methods previously resorted to.

"This man must indeed be dead," said the person who had used the liquor without effect on him.

The clock in the tower had just struck one, and every person thought of retiring; but slight symptoms of returning life being perceptible in the sexton, they still remained.

"God be praised!" exclaimed the sexton awaking; "he is at length restored to rest!"

"Who?" said the colonel.

"Our late schoolmaster."

"What then, that head was actually his?"

"Alas! if you will only promise not to be angry with me, I will confess -It was his."

The colonel then asked him how the idea of disturbing the schoolmaster's corpse in particular came into his head.

"Owing to a diabolical boldness it is commonly believed, that when a child speaks to the head of its deceased parent at the midnight hour, the head comes to life again. I was anxious to prove the fact, but shall never recover from its effects: happily, however, the head is actually restored to rest."

They asked him how he knew it. He answered, that he had seen it all the while he was in a state of lethargy; that as the clock struck one, his wife had finished re-interring the head in its grave. And he described in the most minute manner how she held it.

The curiosity of the company assembled was so much excited by witnessing these inexplicable events that they awaited the return of the servant whom the colonel had dispatched to the sexton's wife. Every thing had happened precisely as he described;- the clock struck one at the very moment the head was laid in the grave.

These events had produced to the spectators a night of much greater terrors than the colonel had prepared for them. Nay, even his imagination was raised to such a pitch, that the least breath of wind, or the slightest noise, appeared to him as a forerunner to some disagreeable visitor from the world of spirits.

He was out of his bed at dawn of day, to look out of his window and see the occasion of the noise which at that hour was heard at the inn-door. He saw the rope-dancers seated in the carriage, about to take their departure. Calzolaro was not with them; but presently afterwards came to the side of the vehicle, where he took leave of them: the children seemed to leave him behind with regret.

The carriage drove off; and the colonel made a signal to Calzolaro to come and speak to him.

"I apprehend," said he to him, when he came in, "that you have taken entire leave of your troop."

"Well, monsieur, ought I not so to do?"

"It appears to me a procedure in which you have acted with as little reflection as the one which tempted you first to join them. You ought rather to have availed yourself of some favourable occasion for withdrawing the little capital that you have in their funds."

"Do you then, monsieur colonel, forget what has happened to me; and that I could not have enjoyed another moment of repose in the society of persons who are only externally men? Every time I recall the scene of last night to my recollection, my very blood freezes in my veins. From this moment I must do all in my power to appease my father's shade, which is now so justly incensed against me. Without much effort I have withdrawn myself from a profession which never had any great charms for me. Reflect only on the misery of being the chief of a troop, who, to earn a scanty morsel of bread, are compelled every moment to risk their lives! -and even this morsel of bread not always attainable. Moreover, I know that the clown belonging to the troop, who is a man devoid of all sentiment, has for a long while aspired to become the chief: and I know that he has for some time been devising various means to remove me from this world; therefore it appears to me that I have not been precipitate in relinquishing my rights to him for a trifling sum of money. I only feel for the poor children; and would willingly have purchased them, to save them from so unhappy a career; but he would not take any price for them. I have only one consolation, which is, the hope that the inhuman treatment they will experience at his hands will induce them to make their escape, and follow a better course of life."

"And what do you purpose doing yourself?"

"I have told you that I shall retire to some obscure corner of Germany, and follow the profession to which my father destined me."

The colonel made him promise to wait a little; and, if possible, he would do something for him.

In the interim, the heiress to his father's property arrived, to have a conference on the subject with him. As soon as he had made known his intentions to her, she entreated him no longer to refuse half the inheritance, or at least to receive it as a voluntary gift on her part. The goodness, the sweetness of this young person, (who was pretty also,) so pleased Calzolaro, that a short time afterwards he asked her hand in marriage. She consented to give it to him. And the colonel then exerted himself more readily in behalf of this man, who had already gained his favour. He fulfilled his wishes, by sending him to a little property belonging to his wife, to follow the profession his father had fixed on for him.

Ere he set off, Calzolaro resumed his German name of Schurster. The good pastor, who had so recently felt indignant at his obstinacy, gave the nuptial benediction to the happy couple in presence of the colonel and his family, who on this occasion gave an elegant entertainment at the *chateau*.

In the evening, a little after sun-set, the bride and bridegroom were walking in the garden, at some little distance from the rest of the company, and appeared plunged in a deep reverie. All on a sudden they looked at each other; for it seemed to them, that some one took a hand of each and united them. They declared, at least, that the idea of this action having taken place came to them both so instantaneously and so involuntarily, that they were astonished at it themselves.

An instant afterwards, they distinctly heard these words:-

"May God bless your union!" pronounced by the voice of Calzolaro's father.

The bridegroom told the colonel, some time afterwards, that without these consolatory words, the terrible apparition which he saw on the memorable night, would assuredly have haunted him all his life, and have empoisoned his happiest moments.

The Death-Bride

THE summer had been uncommonly fine, and the baths crowded with company beyond all comparison: but still the public rooms were scarce ever filled, and never gay. The nobility and military associated only with those of their own rank, and the citizens contented themselves by slandering both parties. So many partial divisions necessarily proved an obstacle to a general and united assembly.

Even the public ball did not draw the *beau-mono* together, because the proprietor of the baths appeared there bedizened with insignia of knight-hood; and this glitter, added to the stiff manners of this great man's family, and the tribe of lackeys in splendid liveries who constantly attended him, compelled the greater part of the company assembled, silently to observe the rules prescribed to them according to their different ranks.

For these reasons the balls became gradually less numerously attended. Private parties were formed, in which it was endeavoured to preserve the charms that were daily diminishing in the public assemblies.

One of these societies met generally twice a week in a room which at that time was usually unoccupied. There they supped, and afterwards enjoyed, either in a walk abroad, or remaining in the room, the charms of unrestrained conversation.

The members of this society were already acquainted, at least by name; but an Italian marquis, who had lately joined their party, was unknown to them, and indeed to every one assembled at the baths.

The title of *Italian* marquis appeared the more singular, as his name, according to the entry of it in the general list, seemed to denote him of Northern extraction, and was composed of so great a number of consonants, that no one could pronounce it without difficulty. His physiognomy and manners likewise presented many singularities. His long and wan visage, his black eyes, his imperious look, had so little of attraction in them, that every one would certainly have avoided him, had he not possessed a fund of entertaining stories, the relation of which proved an excellent antidote to *ennui:* the only drawback against them was, that in general they required rather too great a share of credulity on the part of his auditors.

The party had one day just risen from table, and found themselves but ill inclined for gaiety. They were still too much fatigued from the ball of the preceding evening to enjoy the recreation of walking, although invited so to do by the bright light of the moon. They were even unable to keep up any conversation; therefore it is not to be wondered at, that they were more than usually anxious for the marquis to arrive.

"Where can he be?" exclaimed the countess in an impatient tone.

"Doubtless still at the faro-table, to the no small grief of the bankers," replied Florentine. "This very morning he has occasioned the sudden departure of two of these gentlemen."

"No great loss," answered another.

"To us-," replied Florentine; "but it is to the proprietor of the baths, who only prohibited gambling, that it might be pursued with greater avidity."

"The marquis ought to abstain from such achievements," said the chevalier with an air of mystery. "Gamblers are revengeful, and have generally advantageous connections. If what is whispered be correct, that the marquis is unfortunately implicated in political affairs."

"But," demanded the countess, "what then has the marquis done to the bankers of the gaming-table?"

"Nothing; except that he betted on cards which almost invariably won. And what renders it rather singular; he scarcely derived any advantage from it himself, for he always adhered to the weakest party. But the other punters were not so scrupulous; for they charged their cards in such a manner that the bank broke before the deal had gone round."

The countess was on the point of asking other questions, when the marquis coming in changed the conversation.

"Here you are at last!" exclaimed several persons at the same moment.

"We have," said the countess, "been most anxious for your society; and just on this day you have been longer than usual absent."

"I have projected an important expedition; and it has succeeded to my wishes. I hope by tomorrow there will not be a single gaming-table left here. I have been from one gambling-room to another; and there sufficient post-horses to carry off the ruined bankers."

"And cannot you," asked the countess, "teach us your wonderful art of always winning?"

"It would be a difficult task, my fair lady; and in order to do it, or ensure a fortunate hand, for without that nothing could be done."

"Nay," replied the chevalier, laughing, "Never did I see so fortunate one as yours."

"As you are still very young, my dear chevalier, you have many ties to witness."

Saying these words, the marquis threw on the chevalier so piercing look that the latter cried:

"Will you then cast my nativity?"

"Provided that it is not done to-day," said the countess; "for who knows whether your future destiny will afford us so amusing a history as that which the marquis two days since promised we should enjoy?"

"I did not exactly say *amusing.*"

"But at least full of extraordinary events: and we require some such to draw us from the lethargy which has overwhelmed us all day."

"Most willingly: but first I am anxious to learn whether any of you know aught of the surprising things related of the *Death-Bride.*"

No one remembered to have heard speak of her.

The marquis appeared anxious to add something more by preface; but the countess and the rest of the party so openly manifested their impatience, that the marquis began his narration as follows:

"I had for a long time projected a visit to the count Lieppa, at his estates in Bohemia. We had met each other in almost every country in Europe: attracted *hither* by the frivolity of youth to partake of every pleasure which presented itself, but led *thither* when years of discretion had rendered us more sedate and steady. - At length, in our more advanced age, we ardently desired, ere the close of life, once again to enjoy, by the charms of recollection, the moments of delight which we had passed together. For my part, I was anxious to see the castle of my friend, which was, according to his description, in an extremely romantic district. It was built many hundred of years back by his ancestors; and their successors had preserved it with so much care, that it still maintained its imposing appearance, at the same time it afforded a comfortable abode. The count generally passed the greater part of the year at it with his family, and only returned to the capital at the approach of winter. Being well acquainted with his movements, I did not think it needful to announce my visit; and I arrived at the castle one evening precisely at the time when I knew he would be there; and as I approached it, could not but admire the variety and beauty of the scenery which surrounded it.

"The hearty welcome which I received could not, however, entirely conceal from my observation the secret grief depicted on the countenances of the count, his wife, and their daughter, the lovely Ida. In a short time I discovered that they still mourned the loss of Ida's twin-sister, who had died about a year before. Ida and Hildegarde resembled each other so much, that they were only to be distinguished from each other by a slight mark of a strawberry visible on Hildegarde's neck. Her room, and every thing in it, was left precisely in the same state as when she was alive, and the family were in the habit of visiting it whenever they wished to indulge the sad satisfaction of meditating on the loss of this beloved child. The two sisters had but one heart, one mind: and the parents could not but apprehend that their separation would be but of short duration; they dreaded lest Ida should also be taken from them.

"I did every thing in my power to amuse this excellent family, by entertaining them with laughable anecdotes of my younger days, and by directing their thoughts to less melancholy subjects than that which now wholly occupied them. I had the satisfaction of discovering that my efforts were not ineffectual.

Sometimes we walked in the canton round the castle, which was decked with all the beauties of summer; at other times we took a survey of the different apartments of the castle, and were astonished at their wonderful state of preservation, whilst we amused ourselves by talking over the actions of the past generation, whose portraits hung in a long gallery.

"One evening the count had been speaking to me in confidence, on the subject of his future plans: among other subjects he expressed his anxiety, that Ida (who had already, though only in her sixteenth year, refused several offers) should be happily married; when suddenly the gardener, quite out of breath, came to tell us he had seen the ghost (as he believed, the old chaplain belonging to the castle), who had appeared a century back. Several of the servants followed the gardener, and their pallid countenances confirmed the alarming tidings he had brought.

" 'I believe you will shortly be afraid of your own shadow,' said the count to them. He then sent them off, desiring them not again to trouble him with the like fooleries.

" 'It is really terrible,' said he to me, 'to see to what lengths superstition will carry persons of that rank of life; and it is impossible wholly to undeceive them. From one generation to another an absurd report has from time to time been spread abroad, of an old chaplain's ghost wandering in the environs of the castle; and that he says mass in the chapel, with other idle stories of a similar nature. This report has greatly died away since I came into possession of the castle; but it now appears to me, it will never be altogether forgotten.'

"At this moment the duke de Marino was announced. The count did not recollect ever having heard of him.

"I told him that I was tolerably well acquainted with his family; and that I had lately been present, in Venice, at the betrothing of a young man of that name.

"The very same young man came in while I was speaking. I should have felt very glad at seeing him, had I not perceived that my presence caused him evident uneasiness.

" 'Ah,' said he in a tolerably gay tone, after the customary forms of politeness had passed between us; 'the finding you here, my dear marquis, explains to me an occurrence, which with shame I own caused me a sensation of fear. To my no small surprise, they knew my name in the adjacent district; and as I came up the hill which leads to the castle, I heard it pronounced three times in a voice wholly unknown to me: and in a still more audible tone this strange voice bade me welcome. I now, however, conclude it was yours.'

"I assured him, (and with truth,) that till his name was announced the minute before, I was ignorant of his arrival, and that none of my servants knew him; for that the valet who accompanied me into Italy was not now with me.

" 'And above all,' added I, 'it would be impossible to discover any equipage, however well known to one, in so dark an evening.'

" 'That is what astonishes me,' exclaimed the duke, a little amazed'.
"The incredulous count very politely added, 'that the voice which had told the duke he was welcome, had at least expressed the sentiments of all the family.'

"Marino, ere he said a word relative to the motive of his visit, asked a private audience of me; and confided in me, by telling me that he was come with the intention of obtaining the lovely Ida's hand; and that if he was able to procure her consent, he should demand her of her father.

" 'The countess Apollonia, your bride elect, is then no longer living?" asked I.

" 'We will talk on that subject hereafter,' answered he.

"The deep sigh which accompanied these words led me to conclude that Apollonia had been guilty of infidelity or some other crime towards the duke; and consequently I thought that I ought to abstain from any further questions, which appeared to rend his heart, already so sensibly wounded.

"Yet, as he begged me to become his mediator with the count, in order to obtain from him his consent to the match, I painted in glowing colours the danger of an alliance, which he had no other motive for contracting, than the wish to obliterate the remembrance of a dearly, and without doubt, still more tenderly, beloved object. But he assured me he was far from thinking of the lovely Ida from so blameable a motive, and that he should be the happiest of men if she but proved propitious to his wishes.

"His expressive and penetrating tone of voice, while he said this, lulled the uneasiness that I was beginning to feel; and I promised him I would prepare the count Lieppa to listen to his entreaties, and would give him the necessary information relative to the fortune and family of Marino. But I declared to him at the same time, that I should by no means hurry the conclusion of the affair by my advice, as I was not in the habit of taking upon myself so great a charge as the uncertain issue of a marriage.

"The duke signified his satisfaction at what I said, and made me give (what then appeared to me of no consequence) a promise, that I would not make mention of the former marriage he was on the point of contracting, as it would necessarily bring on a train of unpleasant explanations.

"The duke's views succeeded with a promptitude beyond his most sanguine hopes. His well-proportioned form, and sparkling eyes smoothed the paths of love, and introduced him to the heart of Ida. His agreeable conversation promised to the mother an amiable son-in-law; and the knowledge in rural economy, which he evinced as occasions offered, made the count hope for a useful helpmate in his usual occupations; for since the first day of the duke's arrival he had been prevented from pursuing them.

"Marino followed up these advantages with great ardour; and I was one evening much surprised by the intelligence of his being betrothed, as I did not dream of matters drawing so near a conclusion. They spoke at table of some bridal preparations of which I had made mention just before the duke's arrival at the castle; and the countess asked me whether that young Marino was a near relation of the one who was that very day betrothed to her daughter.

" 'Near enough,' I answered, recollecting my promise. - Marino looked at me with an air of embarrassment.

" 'But, my dear duke,' continued I, 'tell me who mentioned the amiable Ida to you; or was it a portrait, or what else, which caused you to think of looking for a beauty, the selection of whom does so much honour to your taste, in this remote corner; for, if I am not mistaken, you said but yesterday that you had purposed travelling about for another six months; when all at once (I believe while in Paris) you changed your plan, and projected a journey wholly and solely to see the charming Ida?'

" 'Yes, it was at Paris,' replied the duke; 'you are very rightly informed. I went there to see and admire the superb gallery of pictures at the Museum; but I had scarcely entered it, when my eyes turned from the inanimate beauties, and were riveted on a lady whose incomparable features were heightened by an air of melancholy. With fear and trembling I approached her, and only ventured to follow without speaking to her. I still followed her after she quitted the gallery; and I drew her servant aside to learn the name of his mistress. He told it me: but when I expressed a wish to become acquainted with the father of this beauty, he said that was next to impossible while at Paris, as the family were on the point of quitting that city; nay, of quitting France altogether.'

" 'Possibly, however,' said I, 'some opportunity may present itself'. And I looked every where for the lady: but she, probably imagining that her servant was following her closely, had continued to walk on, and was entirely out of sight. While I was looking around for her, the servant had likewise vanished from my view.'

" 'Who was this beautiful lady?' asked Ida, in a tone of astonishment.

" 'What! You really did not then perceive me at the gallery?'

" 'Me!' –'My daughter–!' exclaimed at the same moment Ida and her parents.

" 'Yes, you yourself, mademoiselle. The servant, whom fortunately for me you left at Paris, and whom I met the same evening unexpectedly, *as* my guardian angel, informed me of all; so that after a short rest at home, I was able to come straight hither.'

" 'What a fable!' said the count to his daughter, who was mute with astonishment.

" ' Ida,' he said turning to me 'has never yet been out of her native country; and as for myself, I have not been in Paris these seventeen years.'

"The duke looked at the count and his daughter with similar marks of astonishment visible in their countenances; and conversation would have been entirely at an end, if I had not taken care to introduce other topics: but I had it nearly all to myself.

"The repast was no sooner over, than the count took the duke into the recess of a window; and although I was at a considerable distance, and appeared wholly to fix my attention on a new chandelier, I overheard all their conversation.

" 'What motive,' demanded the count with a serious and dissatisfied air, 'could have induced you to invent that singular scene in the gallery of the Museum at Paris? For according to my judgment, it could in no way benefit you. Since you are anxious to conceal the cause which brought you to ask my daughter in marriage, at least you might have plainly said as much; and though possibly you might have felt repugnance at making such a declaration, there were a thousand ways of framing your answer, without its being needful thus to offend probability.'

" 'Monsieur le count,' replied the duke much piqued; 'I held my peace at table, thinking that possibly you had reasons for wishing to keep secret your and your daughter's journey to Paris. I was silent merely from motives of discretion; but the singularity of your reproaches compels me to maintain what I have said; and, notwithstanding your reluctance to believe the truth, to declare before all the world, that the capital of France was the spot where I first saw your daughter Ida.'

" 'But what if I prove to you, not only by the witness of my servants, but also by that of all my tenants, that my daughter has never quitted her native place?' –

" 'I shall still believe the evidence of my own eyes and ears, which have as great authority over me.'

" 'What you say is really enigmatical,' answered the count in a graver tone: 'your serious manner convinces me you have been the dupe of some illusion; and that you have seen some other person whom you have taken for my daughter. Excuse me, therefore, for having taken up the thing so warmly.'

" 'Another person! What then, I not only mistook another person for your daughter; but the very servant of whom I made mention, and who gave me so exact a description of this castle, was, according to what you say, some other person.'

" 'My dear Marino, that servant was some cheat who knew this castle, and who, God only knows for what motive, spoke to you of my daughter as resembling the lady.'

"'' 'Tis certainly no wish of mine to contradict you; but Ida's features are precisely the same as those which made so deep an impression on me at Paris, and which my imagination has preserved with such scrupulous fidelity.'

"The count shook his head; and Marino continued:-

'What is still more - (but pray pardon me for mentioning a little particularity, which nothing short of necessity would have drawn from me) - while in the gallery, I was standing behind the lady, and the handkerchief that covered her neck was a little disarranged, which occasioned me distinctly to perceive the mark of a small strawberry.'

" 'Another strange mystery!' exclaimed the count, turning pale: 'it appears you are determined to make me believe wonderful stories.'

" 'I have only one question to ask: - Has Ida such a mark on her neck?'

" 'No, monsieur,' replied the count, looking steadfastly at Marino.

" 'No!' exclaimed the latter, in the utmost astonishment.

" 'No, I tell you: but Ida's twin-sister, who resembled her in the most surprising manner, had the mark you mention on her neck, and a year since carried it with her to the grave.'

" 'And yet 'tis only within the last few months that I saw this person in Paris!'

"At this moment the countess and Ida, who had kept aside, a prey to uneasiness, not knowing what to think of the conversation, which appeared of so very important a nature, approached; but the count in a commanding tone ordered them to retire immediately? He then led the duke entirely away into a retired corner of the window, and continued the conversation in so low a voice that I could hear nothing further.

"My astonishment was extreme when, that very same evening, the count gave orders to have Hildegarde's tomb opened in his presence: but he beforehand related briefly what I have just told you, and proposed my assisting the duke and him in opening the grave. The duke excused himself, by saying that the very idea made him tremble with horror; for he could not overcome, especially at night, his fear of a corpse.

"The count begged he would not mention the gallery scene to any one; and above all, to spare the extreme sensibility of the affianced bride from a recital of the conversation they had just had, even if she should request to be informed of it.

"In the mean time the sexton arrived with his lantern. The count and I followed him.

" 'It is morally impossible,' said the count to me, as we walked together, 'that any trick can have been played respecting my daughter's death: the circumstances attendant thereon are but too well known to me. You may readily believe, also, that the affection we bore our poor girl would prevent our running any risk of burying her too soon: but suppose even the possibility of that, and that the tomb had been opened by some avaricious persons, who found, on opening the coffin, that the body became re-animated; no one can believe for a moment that my daughter would not have instantly returned to her parents, who doted on her, rather than have fled to a distant country. This last circumstance puts the matter beyond doubt: for even should it be admitted as a truth, that she was carried by force to some distant part of the world, she would have found a thousand ways of returning. My eyes are, however, about to be convinced that the sacred remains of my Hildegarde really repose in the grave.'

" 'To convince myself!' cried he again, in a tone of voice so melancholy yet loud that the sexton turned his head.

"This movement rendered the count more circumspect; and he continued in a lower tone of voice:

" 'How should I for a moment believe it possible that the slightest trace of my daughter's features should be still in existence, or that the destructive hand of time should have spared her beauty? Let us return, marquis; for who could tell, even were I to see the skeleton, that I should know it from that of an entire stranger, whom they may have placed in the tomb to fill her place?'

"He was even about to give orders not to open the door of the chapel, (at which we were just arrived,) when I represented to him, that were I in his place I should have found it extremely difficult to determine on such a measure; but that having gone thus far, it was requisite to complete the task, by examining whether some of the jewels buried with Hildegarde's corpse were not wanting. I added, that judging by a number of well known facts, all bodies were not destroyed equally soon.

"My representations had the desired effect: the count squeezed my hand; and we followed the sexton, who, by his pallid countenance and trembling limbs, evidently showed that he was unaccustomed to nocturnal employments of this nature.

"I know not whether any of this present company were ever in a chapel at midnight, before the iron doors of a vault, about to examine the succession of leaden coffins enclosing the remains of an illustrious family. Certain it is, that at such a moment the noise of bolts and bars produces such a remarkable sensation, that one is led to dread the sound of the door grating on its hinges; and when the vault is opened, one cannot help hesitating for an instant to enter it.

"The count was evidently seized with these sensations of terror, which I discovered by a stifled sigh; but he concealed his feelings: notwithstanding, I remarked that he dared not trust himself to look on any other coffin than the one containing his daughter's remains. He opened it himself.

" 'Did I not say so?' cried he, seeing that the features of the corpse bore a perfect resemblance to those of Ida. I was obliged to prevent the count, who was seized with astonishment, from kissing the forehead of the inanimate body.

" ' Do not,' I added 'disturb the peace of those who repose in death.' And I used my utmost efforts to withdraw the count immediately from this dismal abode.

"On our return to the castle, we found those persons whom we had left there, in an anxious state of suspense. The two ladies had closely questioned the duke on what had passed; and would not admit as a valid excuse, the promise he had made of secrecy. They entreated us also, but in vain, to satisfy their curiosity.

"They succeeded better the following day with the sexton, whom they sent for privately, and who told them all he knew: but it only tended to excite their anxious wish to learn the subject of the conversation which had occasioned this nocturnal visit to the sepulchral vault.

"As for myself, I dreamt the whole of the following night of the apparition Marino had seen at Paris; I conjectured many things which I did not think fit to communicate to the count, because he absolutely questioned the connection of a superior world with ours. At this juncture of affairs, I with pleasure saw that this singular circumstance, if not entirely forgotten, was at least but rarely and slightly mentioned.

"But I now began to find another cause for anxious solicitude. The duke constantly persisted in refusing to explain himself on the subject of his previous engagement, even when we were alone: and the embarrassment he could not conceal, whenever I made mention of the good qualities that I believed his intended to have possessed, as well as several other little singularities, led me to conclude that Marino's attachment for Apollonia had been first shaken at the picture gallery, at sight of the lovely incognita; and that Apollonia had been forsaken, owing to his yielding to temptations; and that doubtless she could never have been guilty of breaking off an alliance so solemnly contracted.

Foreseeing from this that the charming Ida could never hope to find much happiness in a union with Marino, and knowing that the wedding day was nigh at hand, I resolved to unmask the perfidious deceiver as quickly as possible, and to make him repent his infidelity. An excellent occasion presented itself one day for me to accomplish my designs. Having finished supper, we were still sitting at table; and some one said that iniquity is frequently punished in this world: upon which I observed, that I myself had witnessed striking proofs of the truth of this remark; -when Ida and her mother entreated me to name one of these examples.

" 'Under these circumstances, ladies,' answered I, 'permit me to relate a history to you, which, according to my opinion, will particularly interest you.'

" 'Us!' they both exclaimed. At the same time I fixed my eyes on the duke, who for several days past had evidently distrusted me; and I saw that his conscience had rendered him pale.

" 'That at least is my opinion,' replied I: 'But, my dear Count, will you pardon me, if the supernatural is sometimes interwoven with my narration?'

" 'Very willingly,' answered he smiling: 'and I will content myself with expressing my surprise at so many things of this sort having happened to you, as I have never experienced any of them myself.'

"I plainly perceived that the duke made signs of approval at what he said: but I took no notice of it, and answered the count by saying,

"That all the world have not probably the use of their eyes."

" 'That may be,' replied he, still smiling.

"But," said I to him in a low and expressive voice, "think you an uncorrupted body in the vault is a common phenomenon?"

"He appeared staggered: and 1 thus continued in an under tone of voice:-

" 'For that matter, 'tis very possible to account for it naturally, and therefore it would be useless to contest the subject with you.'

" 'We are wandering from the point,' said the countess a little angrily; and she made me a sign to begin, which I accordingly did, in the following words:-

" 'The scene of my anecdote lies in Venice.'

"'I possibly then may know something of it,' cried the duke, who entertained some suspicions.

" 'Possibly so,' replied I; 'but there were reasons for keeping the event secret: it happened somewhere about eighteen months since, at the period you first set out on your travels.

"The son of an extremely wealthy nobleman, whom I shall designate by the name of Filippo, being attracted to Leghorn by the affairs consequent on his succession to an inheritance, had won the heart of an amiable and lovely girl, called Clara. He promised her, as well as her parents, that ere his return to Venice he would come back and marry her. The moment for his departure was preceded by certain ceremonies, which in their termination were terrible: for after the two lovers had exhausted every protestation of reciprocal affection, Filippo invoked the aid of the spirit of vengeance, in case of infidelity: they prayed even that whichever of the lovers should prove faithful might not be permitted to repose quietly in the grave, but should haunt the perjured one, and force the inconstant party to come amongst the dead, and to share in the grave those sentiments which on earth had been forgotten.

"The parents, who were seated by them at table, remembered their youthful days, and permitted the overheated and romantic imagination of the young people to take its free course. The lovers finished by making punctures in their arms, and letting their blood run into a glass filled with white champagne.

'Our souls shall be inseparable as our blood!' exclaimed Filippo; and drinking half the contents of the glass, he gave the rest to Clara."

At this moment the duke experienced a violent degree of agitation, and from time to time darted such menacing looks at me, that I was led to conclude, that in *his* adventure some scene of a similar nature had taken place. I can however affirm that I related the details respecting Filippo's departure, as they were represented in a letter written by the mother of Clara.

"Who," continued I, "after so many demonstrations of such a violent passion, could have expected the denouement? Filippo's return to Venice happened precisely at the period at which a young beauty, hitherto educated in a distant convent, made her first appearance in the great world: she on a sudden exhibited herself as an angel whom a cloud had till then concealed, and excited universal admiration. Filippo's parents had heard frequent mention of Clara, and of the projected alliance between her and their son; but they thought that this alliance was like many others, contracted one day without the parties knowing why, and broken off the next with equal want of thought; and influenced by this idea, they presented their son to the parents of Camilla, (which was the name of the young beauty,) whose family were of the highest rank.

"They represented to Filippo the great advantages he would obtain by an alliance with her. The Carnival happening just at this period completed the business, by affording him so many favourable opportunities of being with Camilla; and in the end, the remembrance of Leghorn held but very little place in his mind. His letters became colder and colder each succeeding day; and on Clara expressing how sensibly she felt the change, he ceased writing to her altogether, and did every thing in his power to hasten his union with Camilla, who was, without compare, much the handsomer and more wealthy. The agonies poor Clara endured were manifest in her illegible writing, and by the tears which were but too evidently shed over her letters: but neither the one nor the other had any mote influence over the fickle heart of Filippo, than the prayers of the unfortunate girl. Even the menace of coming, according to their solemn agreement, from the tomb to haunt him, and carry him with her to that pave which threatened so soon to enclose her, had but little effect on his mind, which was entirely engrossed with the idea of the happiness he should enjoy in the arms of Camilla.

"The father of the latter (who was my intimate friend) invited me beforehand to the wedding. And although numerous affairs detained him that summer in the city, so that he could not as usual enjoy the pleasures of the country, yet we sometimes went to his pretty villa, situated on the banks of the Brenta; where his daughter's marriage was to be celebrated with all possible splendour.

"A particular circumstance, however, occasioned the ceremony to be deferred for some weeks. The parents of Camilla having been very happy in their own union were anxious that the same priest, who married them, should pronounce the nuptial benediction on their daughter. This priest, who, notwithstanding his great age, had the appearance of vigorous health, was seized with a slow fever which confined him to his bed: however, in time it abated, he became gradually better and better, and the wedding-day was at length fixed. But, as if some secret power was at work to prevent this union, the worthy priest was, on the very day destined for the celebration of their marriage, seized with a feverish shivering of so alarming a nature, that he dared not stir out of the house, and he strongly advised the young couple to select another priest to marry them.

"The parents still persisted in their design of the nuptial benediction being given to their children by the respectable old man who had married them. - They would have certainly spared themselves a great deal of grief, if they had never swerved from their determination. - Very grand preparations had been made in honour of the day; and as they could no longer be deferred, it was decided that they should consider it as a ceremony of solemn affiance. At noon the bargemen attired in their splendid garb awaited the company's arrival on the banks of the canal: their joyous song was soon distinguished, while conducting to the villa, now decorated with flowers, the numerous gondolas containing parties of the best company.

"During the dinner, which lasted till evening, the betrothed couple exchanged rings. At the very moment of their so doing, a piercing shriek was heard, which struck terror into the breasts of all the company, and absolutely struck Filippo with horror. Every one ran to the windows: for although it was becoming dark, each object was visible; but no one was to be seen."

" 'Stop an instant,' said the duke to me, with a fierce smile. - His countenance, which had frequently changed colour during the recital, evinced strong marks of the torments of a wicked conscience.

" 'I am also acquainted with that story, of a voice being heard in the air; it is borrowed from the 'Memoirs of Mademoiselle Clairon;' a deceased lover tormented *her* in this completely original manner. The shriek in her case was followed by a clapping of hands: I hope, monsieur le marquis, that you will not omit that particular in your story.'

" 'And why,' replied I, 'should you imagine that nothing of a similar nature could occur to any one besides that actress? Your incredulity appears to me so much the more extraordinary, as it seems to rest on facts which may lay claim to belief.'

The countess made me a sign to continue; and I pursued my narrative as follows:

"A short time after they had heard this inexplicable shriek, I begged Camilla, facing whom I was sitting, to permit me to look at her ring once more, the exquisite workmanship of which had already been much ad-mired. But it was not on her finger: a general search was made, but not the slightest trace of the ring could be discovered. The company even rose from their seats to look for it, but all in vain.

"Meanwhile, the time for the evening's amusements approached: fireworks were exhibited on the Brenta preceding the ball; the company were masked and got into the gondolas; but nothing was so striking as the silence which reigned during this fete; no one seemed inclined to open their mouth; and scarcely was heard a faint exclamation of *Bravo,* at sight of the fire-works.

"The ball was one of the most brilliant I ever witnessed: the precious stones and jewels, with which the ladies of the party were covered, reflected the lights in the chandeliers with redoubled lustre. The most splendidly attired of the whole was Camilla. Her father, who was fond of pomp, rejoiced in the idea that no one in the assembly was equal to his daughter in splendour or beauty.

"Possibly to satisfy himself of this fact, he made a tour of the room; and returned loudly expressing his surprise, at having perceived on another lady precisely the same jewels which adorned Camilla. He was even weak enough to express a slight degree of chagrin. However, he consoled himself with the idea, that a bouquet of diamonds which was destined for Camilla to wear at supper, would alone in value be greater than all she then had on.

"But as they were on the point of sitting down to table, and the anxious father again threw a look around him, he discovered that the same lady had also a bouquet which appeared to the full as valuable as Camilla's.

"My friend's curiosity could no longer be restrained; he approached, and asked whether it would be too great a liberty to learn the name of the fair mask? But to his great surprise, the lady shook her head, and turned away from him.

"At the same instant the steward came in, to ask whether since dinner there had been any addition to the party, as the covers were not sufficient.

"His master answered, with rather a dissatisfied air, that there were only the same number, and accused his servants of negligence; but the steward still persisted in what he had said.

"An additional cover was placed: the master counted them himself, and discovered that there really was one more in number than he had invited. As he had recently, on account of some inconsiderate expressions, had a dispute with government, he was apprehensive that some spy had contrived to slip in with the company: but as he had no reason to believe, that on such a day as that, any thing of a suspicious nature would be uttered, he resolved, in order to be satisfied respecting so indiscreet a procedure as the introduction of such a person in a family *fete,* to beg every one present to unmask; but in order to avoid the inconvenience likely to arise from such a request, he determined not to propose it till the very last thing.

"Every one present expressed their surprise at the luxuries and delicacies of the table, for it far surpassed every thing of the sort seen in that country, especially with respect to the wines. Still, however, the father of Camilla was not satisfied, and loudly lamented that an accident had happened to his capital red champagne, which prevented his being able to offer his guests a single glass of it.

"The company seemed anxious to become gay, for the whole of the day nothing like gaiety had been visible among them; but no one around where I sat, partook of this inclination, for curiosity alone appeared to occupy their whole attention; I was sitting near the lady who was so splendidly attired, and I remarked that she neither ate nor drank any thing; that she neither addressed nor answered a word to her neighbours, and that she appeared to have her eyes constantly fixed on the affianced couple.

"The rumour of this singularity gradually spread round the room, and again disturbed the mirth which had become pretty general. Each whispered to the other a thousand conjectures on this mysterious personage. But the general opinion was that some unhappy passion for Filippo was the cause of this extraordinary conduct. Those sitting next the unknown, were the first to rise from table, in order to find more cheerful associates, and their places were filled by others who hoped to discover some acquaintance in this silent lady, and obtain from her a more welcome reception; but their hopes were equally futile.

"At the time the champagne was handed round, Filippo also brought a chair and sat by the unknown. She then became somewhat more animated, and turned towards Filippo, which was more than she had done to any one else; and she offered him her glass, as if wishing him to drink out of it.

"A violent trembling seized Filippo, when she looked at him steadfastly.

" 'The wine is red!' cried he, holding up the glass; 'I thought there had been no red champagne.'

" 'Red!' said the father of Camilla, with an air of extreme surprise, approaching him from curiosity.

" 'Look at the lady's glass,' replied Filippo.

'The wine in it is as white as all the rest,' answered Camilla's father; and he called all present to witness it. They every one unanimously declared that the wine was white.

"Filippo drank it not, but quitted his seat; for a second look from his neighbour had caused him extreme agitation. He took the father of Camilla aside, and whispered something to him. The latter returned to the company, saying,

" 'Ladies and gentlemen, I entreat you, for reasons which I will tell you presently, instantly to unmask.'

"As in this request he but expressed in a degree the general wish, every one's mask was off as quick as thought, and each face uncovered, excepting that of the silent lady, on whom every look was fixed, and whose face they were the most anxious to see.

" 'You alone keep on your mask,' said Camilla's father to her, after a short silence: 'May I hope you will also remove yours?'

"She obstinately persisted in her determination of remaining unknown."

"This strange conduct affected the father of Camilla the more sensibly, as he recognised in the others all those whom he had invited to the fete, and found beyond doubt that the mute lady was the one exceeding the number invited. He was, however, unwilling to force her to unmask; because the uncommon splendour of her dress did not permit him any longer to harbour the idea that this additional guest was a spy; and thinking her also a person of distinction, he did not wish to be deficient in good manners. He thought possibly she might be some friend of the family, who, not residing at Venice, but finding on her arrival in that city that he was to give this fete, had conceived this innocent frolic.

"It was thought right, however, at all events to obtain all the information that could be gained from the servants: but none of them knew any thing of this lady; there were no servants of hers there; and those belonging to Camilla's father did not recollect having seen any who appeared to appertain to her.

"What rendered this circumstance doubly strange was, that, as I before mentioned, this lady only put the magnificent bouquet into her bosom the instant previous to her sitting down to supper.

"The whispering, which had generally usurped the place of all conversation, gained each moment more and more ascendancy; when on a sudden the masked lady arose, and walking towards the door beckoned Filippo to follow her; but Camilla hindered him from obeying her signal, for she had a long time observed with what fixed attention the mysterious lady looked at her intended husband; and she had also remarked, that the latter had quitted the stranger in violent agitation; and from all this she apprehended that love had caused him to be guilty of some folly or other. The master of the house, turning a deaf ear to all his daughter's remonstrance's, and a prey to the most terrible fears, followed the unknown (at a distance, it is true); but she was no sooner out of the room than he returned. At this moment, the shriek which they had heard at noon was repeated, but seemed louder from the silence of night, and communicated anew affright to all present. By the time the father of Camilla had returned from the first movement which his fear had occasioned him to make, the unknown was no where to be found.

"The servants in waiting outside the house had no knowledge whatever of the masked lady. In every direction around there were crowds of persons; the river was lined with gondolas; and yet not an individual among them had seen the mysterious female.

"All these circumstances had occasioned so much uneasiness to the whole party, that every one was anxious to return home; and the master of the house was obliged to permit the departure of the gondolas much earlier than he had intended.

"The return home was, *as* might naturally be expected, very melancholy.

"On the following day the betrothed couple were, however, pretty composed. Filippo had even adopted Camilla's idea of the unknown being some one whom love had deprived of reason; and as for the horrible shriek twice repeated, they were willing to attribute it to some people who were diverting themselves; and they decided, that inattention on the part of the servants was the sole cause of the unknown absenting herself without being perceived; and they even at last persuaded themselves, that the sudden disappearance of the ring, which they had not been able to find, was owing to the malice of some one of the servants who had pilfered it.

"In a word, they banished every thing that could tend to weaken these explanations; and only one thing remained to harass them. The old priest, who was to bestow on them the nuptial benediction, had yielded up his last breath; and the friendship which had so intimately subsisted between him and the parents of Camilla, did not permit them in decency to think of marriage and amusements the week following his death.

"The day this venerable priest was buried, Filippo's gaiety received a severe shock; for he learned, in a letter from Clara's mother, the death of that lovely girl. Sinking under the grief occasioned her by the infidelity of the man she had never ceased to love, she died. But to her latest hour she declared she should never rest quietly in her grave, until the perjured man had fulfilled the promise he had made to her.

"This circumstance produced a stronger effect on him than all the imprecations of the unhappy mother; for he recollected that the first shriek (the cause of which they had never been able to ascertain) was heard at the precise moment of Clara's death; which convinced him that the unknown mask could only have been the spirit of Clara.

"This idea deprived him at intervals of his senses

"He constantly carried this letter about him; and with an air of wandering would sometimes draw it from his pocket, in order to reconsider it attentively: even Camilla's presence did not deter him.

"As it was natural to conclude this letter contained the cause of the extraordinary change which had taken place in Filippo, she one day gladly seized the opportunity of reading it, when in one of his absent fits he let it fall from his hands.

"Filippo, struck by the death-like paleness and faintness which overcame Camilla, as she returned him the letter, knew instantly that she had read it. In the deepest affliction he threw himself at her feet, and conjured her to tell him how he must act.

" 'Love me with greater constancy than you did her,' - replied Camilla mournfully.

"With transport he promised to do so. But his agitation became greater and greater, and increased to a most extraordinary pitch the morning of the day fixed for the wedding. As he was going to the house of Camilla's father before it became dark, (from whence he was to take his bride at dawn of day to the church, according to the custom of the country,) he fancied he saw Clara's spirit walking constantly at his side.

"Never was seen a couple about to receive the nuptial benediction, with so mournful an aspect. I accompanied the parents of Camilla, who had requested me to be a witness: and the sequel has made an indelible impression on my mind of the events of that dismal morning.

"We were proceeding silently to the church of the Salutation; when Filippo, in our way thither, frequently requested me to remove the stranger from Camilla's side, for she had evil designs against her.

" 'What stranger?' I asked him

" 'In God's name, don't speak so loud,' replied he; 'for you cannot but see how anxious she is to force herself between Camilla and me.'

" 'Mere chimera, my friend; there are none but yourself and Camilla.'

" 'Would to Heaven my eyes did not deceive me!' – 'Take care that she does not enter the church,' added he, as we arrived at the door.

" 'She will not enter it, rest assured,' said I: and to the great astonishment of Camilla's parents I made a motion as if to drive some one away.

"We found Filippo's father already in the church; and as soon as his son perceived him, he took leave of him as if he was going to die. Camilla sobbed; and Filippo exclaimed:-

" 'There's the stranger; she has then got in.'

"The parents of Camilla doubted whether under such circumstances the marriage ceremony ought to be begun.

"But Camilla, entirely devoted to her love, cried: - 'These chimeras of fancy render my care and attention the more necessary.'

"They approached the altar. At that moment a sudden gust of wind blew out the wax-tapers. The priest appeared displeased at their not having shut the windows more securely; but Filippo exclaimed: 'The windows! See you not, then, that there is one here who blew out the wax-tapers purposely?'

"Every one looked astonished: and Filippo cried, as he hastily disengaged his hand from that of Camilla, - 'Don't you see, also, that she is tearing me away from my intended bride?'

"Camilla fell fainting into the arms of her parents; and the priest declared, that under such peculiar circumstances it was impossible to proceed with the ceremony.

"The parents of both attributed Filippo's state to mental derangement. They even supposed he had been poisoned; for an instant after, the unfortunate man expired in most violent convulsions. The surgeons who opened his body could not, however, discover any grounds for this suspicion.

"The parents, who as well as myself were informed by Camilla of the subject of these supposed horrors of Filippo, did every thing in their power to conceal this adventure: yet, on talking over all the circumstances, they could never satisfactorily explain the apparition of the mysterious mask at the time of the wedding fete. And what still appeared very surprising was, that the ring lost at the country villa was found amongst Camilla's other jewels, at the time of their return from church."

" 'This is, indeed, a wonderful history!' said the count. His wife uttered a deep sigh: and Ida exclaimed, -

" 'It has really made me shudder.'

'That is precisely what every betrothed person ought to feel who listens to such recitals,' answered I, looking steadfastly at the duke, who, while I was talking, had risen and sat down again several times; and who, from his troubled look, plainly shewed that he feared I should counteract his wishes.

" 'A word with you!' he whispered me, as we were retiring to rest: and he accompanied me to my room. 'I plainly perceive your generous intentions; this history invented for the occasion —'

" 'Hold!' said I to him in an irritated tone of voice: 'I was eye-witness to what you have just heard. How then can you doubt its authenticity, without accusing a man of honour of uttering a falsehood?'

" 'We will talk on this subject presently,' replied he in a tone of raillery. 'But tell me truly from whence you learnt the anecdote relative to mixing the blood with wine? - I know the person from whose life you borrowed this idea.'

" 'I do assure you that I have taken it from no one's life but Filippo's; and yet there may be similar stories - as of the shriek, for instance. But even this singular manner of irrevocably affiancing themselves may have presented itself to any two lovers.'

" 'Perhaps so! Yet one could trace in your narration many traits resembling another history.'

" 'That is very possible: all love-stories are founded on the same stock, and cannot deny their parentage.

" 'No matter,' replied Marino; 'but I desire that from henceforth you do not permit yourself to make any allusion to my past life; and still less that you relate certain anecdotes to the count. On these conditions, and only on these conditions, do I pardon your former very ingenious fiction.'

" 'Conditions! - forgiveness! - And do you dare thus to talk to me? This is rather too much. Now take my answer: To-morrow morning the count shall know that you have been already affianced, and what you now exact.'

" 'Marquis, if you dare -,'

" 'Oh! oh! - Yes, I dare do it; and I owe it to an old friend. The impostor who dares accuse me of falsehood shall no longer wear his deceitful mask in this house.'

"Passion had, spite of my endeavours, carried me so far, that a duel became inevitable. The duke challenged me. And we agreed, at parting, to meet the following morning in a neighbouring wood with pistols.

"In effect, before daylight we each took our servant and went into the forest.

Marino, remarking that I had not given any orders in case of my being killed, undertook to do so for me; and accordingly he told my servant what to do with my body, as if every thing was already decided. He again addressed me ere we shook hands; 'For,' said he, 'the combat between us must be very unequal. I am young,' added he; 'but in many instances my hand has proved a steady one. I have not, it is true, absolutely killed any man; but I have invariably hit my adversary precisely on the part I intended. In this instance, however, I must, for the first time, kill my man, as it is the only effectual method of preventing your annoying me further; unless you will give me your word of honour not to discover any occurrences of my past life to the count, in which case I consent to consider the affair as terminated here.'

"As you may naturally believe, I rejected his proposition.

'As it must be so,' replied he, 'recommend your soul to God.' We prepared accordingly.

'It is your first fire,' he said to me.

" 'I yield it to you,' answered I.

"He refused to fire first. I then drew the trigger, and caused the pistol to drop from his hand. He appeared surprised: but his astonishment was great indeed, when, after taking up another pistol, he found he had missed me. He pretended to have aimed at my heart; and had not even the possibility of an excuse; for he could not but acknowledge that no sensation of fear on my part had induced me to move, and baulk his aim.

"At his request I fired a second time; and again aimed at his pistol which he held in his left hand: and to his great astonishment it dropped also; but the ball had passed so near his hand, that it was a good deal bruised.

"His second fire having passed me, I told him I would not fire again; but that, as it was possible the extreme agitation of his mind had occasioned him to miss me twice, I proposed adjusting matters.

"Before he had time to refuse my offer, the count who had suspicions that all was not right, was between us, with his daughter. He complained loudly of such conduct on the part of his guests; and demanded some explanation on the cause of our dispute. I then developed the whole business in presence of Marino, whose evident embarrassment convinced the count and Ida of the truth of the reproaches his conscience made him.

"But the duke soon availed himself of Ida's affection, and created an entire change in the count's mind; who that very evening said to me, -

" 'You are right; I certainly ought to take some decided step, and send the duke from my house: but what could win the Apollonia whom he has abandoned, and whom he will never see again? Added to which, he is the only man for whom my daughter has ever felt a sincere attachment. Let us leave the young people to follow their own inclinations: the countess perfectly coincides in this opinion; and adds, that it would hurt her much were this handsome Venetian to be driven from our house. How many little infidelities and indiscretions are committed in the world and excused, owing to particular circumstances?'

'But it appears to me, that in the case in point, these particular circumstances are wanting,' answered I. However, finding the count persisted in his opinion, I said no more.

"The marriage took place without any interruption: but still there was very little of gaiety at the feast, which usually on these occasions is of so splendid and jocund a nature. The ball in the evening was dull; and Marino alone danced with extraordinary glee.

'Fortunately, monsieur le marquis,' said he in my ear, quitting the dance for an instant and laughing aloud, 'there are no ghosts or spirits here, as at your Venetian wedding.

" 'Don't,' I answered, putting up my finger to him, 'rejoice too soon: misery is slow in its operations; and often is not perceived by us blind mortals till it treads on our heels.'

"Contrary to my intention, this conversation rendered him quite silent; and what convinced me the more strongly of the effect it had made on him, was, the redoubled vehemence with which the duke again began dancing.

"The countess in vain entreated him to be care of his health: and all Ida's supplications were able to obtain was, a few minutes' rest to take breath when he could no longer go on.

"A few minutes after, I saw Ida in tears, which did not appear as if occasioned by joy; and she quitted the ball-room. I was standing as close to the door as I am to you at this moment; so that I could not for an instant doubt its being really Ida: but what appeared to me very strange was, that in a few seconds I saw her come in again with a countenance as calm as possible. I followed her, and remarked that she asked the duke to dance; and was so far from moderating his violence, that she partook of and even increased it by her own example. I also remarked, that as soon as the dance was over the duke took leave of the parents of Ida, and with her vanished through a small door leading to the nuptial apartment.

"While I was endeavouring to account in my own mind how it was possible for Ida so suddenly to change her sentiments, a conference in an undertone took place at the door of the room, between the count and his valet.

"The subject was evidently a very important one, as the greatly incensed looks of the count towards his gardener evinced, while *he* confirmed, as it appeared, what the valet had before said.

"I drew near the trio, and heard, that at a particular time the church organ was heard to play, and that the whole edifice had been illuminated within, until twelve o'clock, which had just struck.

"The count was very angry at their troubling him with so silly a tale, and asked why they did not sooner inform him of it. They answered, that everyone was anxious to see how it would end. The gardener added, that the old chaplain had been seen again; and the peasantry, who lived near the forest, even pretended that they had seen the summit of the mountain which overhung their valley illuminated, and spirits dance around it.

'Very well!' exclaimed the count with a gloomy air; 'so all the old idle trash is resumed: the Death-Bride' is also, I hope, going to play her part.'

"The valet having pushed aside the gardener, that he might not still further enrage the count, I put in my word; and said to the count, 'You might at least listen to what they have to say, and learn what it is they pretend to have seen.'

" 'What is said about the Death-Bride?' said I to the gardener.

"He shrugged up his shoulders.

" 'Was I not right?' cried the count: 'here we are then, and must listen to this ridiculous tale. All these things are treasured in the memory of these people, and constantly afford subjects and phantoms to their imaginations. - Is it permitted to ask under what form? —'

'Pray pardon me,' replied the gardener; 'but it resembled the deceased Mademoiselle Hildegarde. She passed close to me in the garden, and then came in to the castle.'

'O!' said the count to him, 'I beg, in future you will be a little more circumspect in your fancies, and leave my daughter to rest quietly in the tomb. - 'Tis well-'

"He then made a signal to his servants, who went out.

" 'Well! My dear marquis!' said he to me.

" 'Well?'

" 'Your belief in stories will not, surely, carry you so far as to give credence to my Hildegarde's spirit appearing?'

" 'At least it may have appeared to the gardener only. Do you recollect the adventure in the Museum at Paris?'

" 'You are right: that again was a pretty invention, which to this moment I cannot fathom. Believe me; I should sooner have refused my daughter to the duke for his having been the fabricator of so gross a story, than for his having forsaken his first love.'

" 'I see very plainly that we shall not easily accord on this point; for if my ready belief appears strange to you, your doubts seem to me incomprehensible.'

"The company assembled at the castle, retired by degrees; and I alone was left with the count and his lady, when Ida came to the room-door, clothed in her ball-dress, and appeared astonished at finding the company had left.

" 'What can this mean?' demanded the countess. Her husband could not find words to express his astonishment.

" 'Where is Marino?' exclaimed Ida.

" 'Do you ask us where he is?' replied her mother; 'did we not see you go out with him through that small door?'

" 'That could not be; - you mistake.'

"No, no; my dear child! A very short time since you were dancing with singular vehemence; and then you both went out together.'

" 'Me! My mother?'

" 'Yes, my dear Ida: how is it possible you should have forgotten all this?'

" 'I have forgotten nothing, believe me.'

" 'Where then have you been all this time?'

" 'In my sister's chamber,' said Ida.

"I remarked that at these words the count became somewhat pale; and Ida's fearful eye caught mine: he however said nothing. The countess, fearing that her daughter was deceiving her, said to her in an afflicted tone of voice:-

" 'How could so singular a fancy possess you on a day like this?'

" 'I cannot account for it; and only know, that all on a sudden I felt an oppression at my heart, and fancied that all I wanted was Hildegarde. At the same time I felt a firm belief that I should find her in her room playing on her guitar; for which reason I crept thither softly.'

" 'And did you find her there?'

" 'Alas! no: but the eager desire that I felt to see her, added to the fatigue of dancing, so entirely overpowered me, that I seated myself on a chair, where I fell fast asleep.'

" 'How long since did you quit the room?'

" 'The clock in the tower struck the three-quarters past eleven just as I entered my sister's room.'

" 'What does all this mean?' said the countess to her husband in a low voice: 'she talks in a connected manner; and yet I know, that as the clock struck three-quarters past eleven, I entreated Ida on this very spot to dance more moderately.'

" 'And Marino?' - asked the count.

" 'I thought, as I before said, that I should find him here.'

" 'Good God!' exclaimed the mother, 'she raves: but the duke - Where is he then?'

" 'What then, my good mother?' said Ida with an air of great disquiet, while leaning on the countess.

"Meanwhile the count took a wax-taper, and made a sign for me to follow him. A horrible spectacle awaited us in the bridal-chamber, whither he conducted me. We there found the duke extended on the floor. There did not appear the slightest signs of life in him; and his features were distorted in the most frightful manner.

"Imagine the extreme affliction Ida endured when she heard this recital, and found that all the resources of the medical attendants were employed in vain.

"The count and his family could not be roused from the deep consternation which threatened to overwhelm them. A short time after this event, some business of importance occasioned me to quit their castle; and certainly I was not sorry for the excuse to get away.

"But ere I left that county, I did not fail to collect in the village every possible information relative to the Death-Bride; whose history unfortunately, in passing from one mouth to another, experienced many alterations. It appeared to me, however, upon the whole, that this affianced bride lived in this district, about the fourteenth or fifteenth century. She was a young lady of noble family, and she had conducted herself with so much perfidy and ingratitude towards her lover, that he died of grief; but afterwards, when she was about to marry, he appeared to her the night of her intended wedding, and she died in consequence. And it is said, that since that time, the spirit of this unfortunate creature wanders on earth in every possible shape; particularly in that of lovely females, to render their lovers inconstant.

"As it was not permitted for her to appear in the form of any living being, she always chose amongst the dead those who the most strongly resembled them. It was for this reason she voluntarily frequented the galleries in which were hung family portraits. It is even reported that she has been seen in galleries of pictures open to public inspection. Finally, it is said, that, as a punishment for her perfidy, she will wander till she finds a man whom she will in vain endeavour to make swerve from his engagement; and it appears, they added, that as yet she had not succeeded.

"Having inquired what connection subsisted between this spirit and the old chaplain (of whom also I had heard mention), they informed me, that the fate of the last depended on the young lady, because he had assisted her in her criminal conduct. But no one was able to give me any satisfactory information concerning the voice which had called the duke by his name, nor on the meaning of the church being illuminated at night; and why the grand mass was chanted. No one either knows how to account for the dance on the mountain's top in the forest.

"For the rest," added the marquis, "you will own, that the traditions are admirably adapted to my story, and may, to a certain degree, serve to fill up the gaps; but I am not enabled to give a more satisfactory explanation. I reserve for another time a second history of this same *Death-Bride;* I only heard it a few weeks since: it appears to me interesting; but it is too late to begin to-day, and indeed, even now, I fear that I have intruded too long on the leisure of the company present by my narrative.

He had just finished these words, and some of his auditors (though all thanked him for the trouble he had taken) were expressing their disbelief of the story, when a person of his acquaintance came into the room in a hurried manner, and whispered something in his ear. Nothing could be more striking than the contrast presented by the bustling and uneasy air of the newly arrived person while speaking to the marquis, and the calm air of the latter while listening to him.

"Haste, I pray you," said the first (who appeared quite out of patience at the marquis's *sang-froid):* "In a few moments you will have cause to repent this delay."

"I am obliged to you for your affecting solicitude," replied the marquis; who in taking up his hat, appeared more to do, as all the rest of the party were doing, in preparing to return home, than from any anxiety of hastening away.

"You are lost," said the other, as he saw an officer enter the room at the head of a detachment of military, who inquired for the marquis. The latter instantly made himself known to him.

"You are my prisoner," said the officer. The marquis followed him, after saying Adieu with a smiling air to all the party, and begging they would not feel any anxiety concerning him.

"Not feel anxiety!" replied he whose advice he had neglected "I must inform you, that they have discovered that the marquis has been detected in a connection with very suspicious characters; and his death-warrant may be considered as signed. I came in pity to warn him of his danger, for possibly he might then have escaped; but from his conduct since, I can scarcely imagine he is in his proper senses.

The party, who were singularly affected by this event, were conjecturing a thousand things, when the officer returned, and again asked for the marquis. "He just now left the room with you," answered some one of the company.

"But he came in again."

"We have seen no one."

"He has then disappeared," replied the officer, smiling: he searched every corner for the marquis, but in vain. The house was thoroughly examined, but without success; and the following day the officer quitted the baths with his soldiers, without his prisoner, and very much dissatisfied.

The Ghost of the Departed

Julien, the only child of Baron Soller, stood to inherit the feudal estate and three considerable houses in the local town. Consequently she had more admirers than would normally be expected for a well-bred girl with an especially lovely face. As a result, at the age of seventeen, she had already had the opportunity to gently evade various marriage proposals by way of answers with double-meanings and to choose her own way in life.

Her father, who was the cause her independence, was happy to have such an intelligent daughter.

"You don't know Julien!" He said confidently, as someone mentioned that they had observed her particular friendliness with Doctor Hess. He believed that the girl's hopes did not extend beyond the boundaries of his quiet and comfortable house. He forgot that the wishes of youth are very different from that of their elders and that a well cultivated, problem-less life stimulates, rather than softens, the search for fulfilment.

So he was even more surprised when a letter from the Doctor, which was definitely for Julien, arrived in her absence and due to the stupidity of the messenger was delivered to Herr Soller. The hand-written address was in a male hand and the father waited impatiently for the return of his daughter.

Her shock, as he gave her the letter, caused him to snatch back the letter, open it and read about the undying love which Dr Gustav Hess repeatedly expressed in the letter. A strict examination followed an even stricter forbidding. Julien had to promise a great deal just keep the peace for the moment!

The interrupted correspondence, the news of which the teary eyed girl could only give to her love from her window, disposed the unquiet heart of the Doctor to speak with Baron Soller. Gustav asked for Julien's hand in marriage formally, which was, not any less formally, denied. This was puzzling since Dr. Hess was independent, had good assets, a good reputation and manners and possessed all that his request should require. Even the small scar of honour on his cheek, caused by a duel did not cause bad feelings amongst people for it was generally known that the argument had not been induced by him.

Julien hoped, in vain, that her father, whose opinions were usually quite pliable, would not stand in the way of her permanent happiness. Everything was done, by herself and the doctor, to try and win him over to accept their proposed relationship.

After a great deal of fruitless attempts it seemed to the girl that it was conceivable, thanks to his stubbornness, and she was not wrong in that thought, that there was little hope that she would be able to carry out her wish during her father's lifetime. Baron Soller was, since his illness, gifted with the unfortunate ability to see ghosts. He had, bit by bit, in spite of doctor Jung, built his own psychological system in which those people who appeared, as ghosts, during their lifetime were thought to have a highly suspicious character.

Julien was particularly worried, that the ghost of her lover must have been seen by her father and left her intelligence no rest until she understood the situation fully. Immediately, in the night that the letter was intercepted, Doctor Hess, dressed completely in his everyday suit, appeared by the bed of Baron Soller.

Only one desperate method, which her modesty rebelled against, occurred to Julien, and her love would not rest until she had applied it. She gave her father the wrong impression that she, because of his rage and her heart, was tempted and that she then opened the door to the doctor at night. Consequently it was the doctor himself and not his ghost that Baron Soller had seen. She also told him how she had got possession of the key to the house and entrance-room, in such detail and with so much sincerity, until no doubt about it remained.

The result demonstrated that Julien understood how to choose her methods. Even though he was angry with the events, the father's aversion to the doctor eased. Julie informed her lover of the fact. He repeated his request for her hand in marriage and Herr Soller, who seemed doubtful about the possibility of protecting his daughter from a lover to whom she would open his household door, gave his permission.

Unfortunately, eight days before the wedding, the father saw the ghost again. This time the ghost seer paid such attention to the doors that Julien was unable to repeat her former deception. Herr Soller now wanted to call off the wedding. A formal prophesy, which showed his daughters future unhappiness could not fail to leave an impression. But the lover knew how to push any such prophesy away from Julien's heart. The engagement had been made public and the pair held the father to his word that he had earlier given. He knew that everyone would have considered his excuse for a sudden change of mind the result of some mental illness and he could think of no valid reason. Finally he agreed but nevertheless refused to be a witness to the wedding.

However, once this was over the normal relationship between father and daughter was restored. He acknowledged the pair and admitted to the young woman that, until now, his worries about her husband had been unfounded.

Doctor Hess renounced his medical practice, to which he had devoted himself, or rather limited it to a number of friends whom he served from special goodwill.

Thus the newly-wedded couple were able to follow their love and passion which they did so to their hearts content. They hung on every dream with heated passion, had endless conversations and occasionally Herr Soller's ghost seeing was also mentioned. Occasionally the hopes of the beloved were filled with the possibility of resurrection after death. The couple would now not refuse the possibility that the ghosts, which Baron Soller occasionally saw, had perhaps some form of being even though the results which he attributed to them were rather questionable. Dr. Hess knew the story of two lovers who promised each other, after death, not to leave one another and that the husband, who died first, remained true unto the smallest detail, of their promise and returned. The mentioning that such should happen to them too was made by Julien and very warmly repeated by Dr Hess. They attempted to collect all sorts of strange opinions which had been printed about the spiritual world and even a few very peculiar handwritten theories became part of their strange collection of reading material.

Initially the couple had a suspicion with regards to a possibility, which now led them to the belief of a certainty of the matter and with the help of various gathered hypotheses they arrived at their own theory in a similar way as had Baron Soller. Following their theory a couple who are truly in love could not be separated by death. The first of the couple to pass away would surround the remaining partner in the form of a protective guardian angel until their later reunification.

Fortunately their new obsession gradually became worn away by the passage of time and life. But the human weaknesses which each noticed in the other disturbed the idea of togetherness that each had had for the other. So much so that, after Julien's first pregnancy, their idea of returning from the shadow-lands was completely forgotten. Their otherwise un-wandering love became, with every month, more wandering. And even though the baby, who had seemed to have become the complete reason for his mothers life was carried to the grave by illness Dr Hess did not seem to be moved towards a closer bond with his wife.

The couple who had been so happy to be a unity began to reaffirm their individuality and though neither could accuse the other of being untrue they were both of differing opinions as to the cause when looking back.

After three years had passed the inner bond that had joined them seemed completely gone. Only, perhaps, an outer bond kept them together. The lies against the fathers prophesy seemed now to punish them and their friends, who could still not forget the example of their love on the wedding-day, also gave them little to laugh about.

Doctor Hess, who, as previously noted, out of love for a restful and enjoyable life had not used his medical knowledge for financial gain, had spent the main part of the summers of the first two years at a well known bathing spot with Julien.

On the third summer he intended to go again to this bathing spot. It was Julien who refused to accompany him by claiming that she still felt weakened from the second unsuccessful birth. It did not bother her, that her husband, as his smile proved, could see through the falsehood of her pretext.

Only after his departure did it occur to her that something was not right; something over which he had, for months, complained about and which she had put down to his mood swings. If it was true! If, far away amongst strangers, he was to become ill! The thought almost had her ordering a post-horse.

Happy company pushed away clouds from her youthful mind, and she called herself an idiot to have such worries of her husband who was, in the presence of friends, recovering from a ennui which had been caused by her presence.

All in all she did not mind the current loneliness. Many of the considerations which she had to make when her husband was around could now be dropped. She was currently only accountable to herself and the law of morals. She had begun to think, with some fear, about the impending change of this situation, when a letter from the doctor arrived postponing his return by three weeks.

She welcomed the situation but was also unhappy that Dr. Hess did not even mention a reason for his prolonged absence.

After a week passed she received a note from her husband's brother who was a well respected judge in a distant county who, as she had now discovered undertook a long journey to the bathing spot to see his beloved and only brother after a long abstinence. The extremely dangerous illness of her husband, that the note mentioned, had an unnerving effect and just as Julie was ready to make an urgent departure she received a second note and discovered that the first one was only meant to prepare her for the message informing her of his death. A sudden consumption was the cause of his untimely death.

Since he had many friends at this bathing spot, mainly due to his entertaining talents, his funeral was very touching and emotional. The brother, who wrote all this, explained to the widow that he was planning to tell her all this in person when he was suddenly and unexpectedly called away due to his job. He remembered, that her husband had mentioned, briefly in a conversation, that her truso didn't even approach one third of his wealth and that was why he had put in writing his wishes that she should receive this third in money and bonds.

Julie felt so upset by the death that, at this unfortunate moment, economic details seemed somewhat unworthy. Though unintentional, she developed a strong dislike towards the author of the letter for considering it worthwhile to mention in the first days of her bereavement.

The fact that she had not taken her husband's minor complaints seriously, something which she remembered shortly after his departure, tortured her. Every beautiful moment of her love returned from within her memory,
particularly the long forgotten scene in which they had promised each other to appear after death. Not without feverish fear did she return in the evening from her father's house to the dusky loneliness.

Once she was undressed her maid intended to leave but she called her back. However the decision to have her keep guard was brushed away immediately and the maid was sent away without her knowing why she had been called back. Julien didn't want to restrain the ghost of her husband by the presence of a witness though she was shaking so much that she just about managed to reach the bed. She wished for no other protection than sleep.

Although she shut her eyes very tight and closed the bed curtains which she generally kept open, she could not find sleep. Indeed it was strangely noisy around her, more so than one would expect in such a lonely room. When finally, full of fear, she turned her face towards the wall, prepared for anything, opening the curtains and looking up, the light gave a strange uneven spark and created, on one side of the room, a dark puzzling shadow which the trembling Julien had never seen before.

This shadow seemed very suspicious to her and the longer she looked at it as more mobile it became. The candle's flame flickered in such a way as to suggest that something was influencing it.

What unnerved Julien even more was the sound of the grandfather clock, not far away from the bed, whose repetitiveness was not disturbed in the slightest by the strange events. She felt brave enough to make the clock stop but just as she got herself up the sound of the midnight chimes sounded to her like a ghostly call and threw her back. It was as if the chime ripped her tightly shut eyes open, and this only so that she could see how, out of the accursed shadows the ghostly figure of her husband appeared and walked silently towards her bed.

This was the last moment of her consciousness and, on the next morning, she lay with a burning fever.

Only after a few months did she completely recover. Her father had now become very keen to discover more about the ghost whose appearance she had mentioned during the height of the fever attacks. Julie did not remember anything about her remarks and intentionally avoided mentioning the night which led to her illness.

Her first thought after recovering was to visit the grave of her husband by way of a pilgrimage to the bathing spot. She felt touched and thankful when looking at the stone which had been placed by a few friends upon his grave. Her husband, as she discovered now, died as a result of his profession. It was an illness that he had contracted from a helpless patient, who he had taken in to his flat out of pure mercy, which had pushed him into the grave. It had not been mentioned to her that his death had been accelerated by a fall out of bed, only the fact that many people had heard about it meant that it could not stay hidden from her for she spoke to too many about her dead husband.

Since the bathing spot, except for the cemetery, was not a suitable place for grieving she was somewhat pleased with the fact that her female companion did not get on with the local water and thus found her decision to depart quite agreeable. The return home offered Julien some distraction but nothing to put her mind at rest.

Her long ailing father became bed-bound and the doctors did not hide from her that his suffering would probably end only with his death. Thus, caring for him meant a lot to her. The knowledge that a beloved one may very soon die gives our love a previously undiscovered power. Julien did not leave the room of her father. Anyone who wanted to see her had to also visit the ailing patient and, because of this reason, the old man had more visits from young men who were keen to change their bachelor life into a purposeful one.

The silent but constant present attention that the beautiful widow gave to the wishes of her patient could not have failed to increase the interest of those young men. For what would such a being, who withdraws from all the pleasures of youth in order to fulfill the wishes of a hopelessly ill patient and put up with his moods; what would such a being be able to offer to a husband? But although some of them laid their intention open, and some of them could be called a good catch, and it would have been only up to her to choose, she did not pick any of them. After ten months of suffering her father finally passed away and was buried.

Following his death she attached herself to some social families but not because she was seeking for opportunities to escape her grieving. The memories of the first weeks of her marriage stood before her in the brightest and most vivid colours. At those times their love for each other had been so great that she did not dare to hope for a similar one in the future. Moreover she did not dare to invite a reflection of her past happiness back into her life because the price she would have to pay for the loss of her independency seemed too high.

She admitted this to a few suitors without holding back, so that her decision to remain a widow caused some of them to create a humorous poem that made a mockery of her. Her beauty, which had suffered due to lack of sleep whilst looking after her ill father, had reached full blossom again and her mind regained the former agility.

The fact that she had let her husband travel alone to the bathing spot still put her at unease even though the ghost had not appeared again since the first time.

She now, at times, even doubted whether it was his ghost she had seen and thought that it was more likely a fantasy driven by her guilt and oncoming illness. She was not pleased with her fear in any case. Even so, if it had have been a ghost, she said, it would have been more believable that it would be her good and beloved husband, sticking to his previous promise to return, rather than some fearful apparition.

Her life which had recovered, bit by bit, now lost some social pleasure, due to the marriage of her maid who was a most caring and loyal servant. The servant had grown up with Julien and had even had the pleasure to take part in some of her education. She wished to marry someone who neither matched her position in society nor education.

Julien allowed her do so, and even organised the wedding, but continued contact with one who embarrassed herself was not possible for it threatened to pull Julien down into an uneducated circle. The lonelier she felt the more attention she paid to her imagination and images of her first days of love. It went so far that, on a few occasions she wished that her dead husband would return, in the shape of a ghost, so that he could see how she gained pleasure from reading his passionate letters or how she pressed a picture or some memento upon her breast. In brief her whole life was no longer independent but wholly focussed upon her previous relationship.

With these feelings she went to sleep once again just as the carriages raced down to the mask ball to which she had refused an urgent invitation

She may have slept for a few hours and when her eyes opened again, in that same moment she saw a figure in the background of the adjacent room moving towards her very slowly. The long yearned for shadow which could not fail to be recognised.

The fear that she could have disturbed her husband in his deathly peace, by wishing for him to return, came upon her and robbed her of any pleasure from the appearance. Speechless, the fear took her breath away and she closed her eyes even though the shadow was in the room next door.

Gradually, as the fear waned, she opened her eyelids to see whether the apparition was close to her bed. Julien remained in this fearful expectation for some time until the figure finally moved away silently.

Not until half an hour later did she feel brave enough to move and pull the bell. She pulled it three times, the last time particularly hard, without gaining any reaction from the maid.

The clock chimed two and she got up to search for the maid but only found an empty bed. The cook and the servant both slept on the upper floor where there was no bell. That the new maid lived an immoral life was known to Julien. Without doubt she had left the house in the hope not to be missed. Surprising then that the widow found the outer door locked!

On the next morning the maid's tired eyes said it all and she admitted to Julien, later on, that she had most thoroughly participated in the masked ball. Since Julie had previously repetitively forbid her to disappear at night she was dismissed and sent away. Julie was able, on the same day, to find a new maid who settled in far better than the three she had employed since her first maid had got married.

Every night the widow suffered from a fear like that which may accompany a bad fever. The sound of every tiny movement of air sent a judder though her whole body. Her eyes refused to recognise the figure of her dead husband but her ear heard his every movement. She now asked for her father's forgiveness for having doubted his visions. She did not seek to hide the appearances from anybody but would become very angry with anyone who had any doubts about the spectre that stood in front of her bed. She would not allow anyone to doubt the capability of her eyes and ears. She now mentioned the earlier appearance of the ghost just after her husband's death, and that initially she had not said a word to anybody as she thought that it was a symptom of her feverish condition. She asked whether signs of madness were apparent upon her. Even natural explanations, which were dared to be given, often upset her. Somebody suggested that a lover of the previous beautiful and liberal maid may have gone to the wrong room and that this was even more likely since the so called ghost appeared in ordinary casual clothes which would have not suited that of a ghost.

Julien's answer to this was that the maid's lover had received a key for the house and flat so that they would have found the maid on the other side of the room and that the outer door was really locked. She would not allow anyone to doubt it.

She quashed suggestions regarding the ghost's costume; particularly the suggestion that a bodiless creature would have had to take on natural bodily features in order to be recognisable and, as she added with passion, she would swear an oath that there was no difference between the ghostly appearance and that of her dead husband. Her eagle eye even saw clearly the duelling scar upon his cheek.

Julien spoke about this so openly and so convincingly that she had a crowd of followers and her seeing ghosts became the topic of many a conversations. It would have thus been surprising if the whole thing should have escaped the newspaper.

Although the gossip, anonymously distributed amongst the people, was full of untruths our heroin, whose name was not mentioned in the papers, she felt that the story was reported without upsetting anyone. Even mockery from various people could not shake her belief. Since her new maid began sleeping in her room she neither saw nor heard anything unusual. With the short summer nights her bravery returned, to some extent, and without the slightest fear she spent every night alone again. Nevertheless her belief in the reality of the appearance had not wavered nor weakened.

Towards the end of the summer in a house belonging to part of her social circle she met, quite unexpectedly, a highly respected friend of her late husband who she had not seen for a long time. She was very pleased to see the man who was wonderfully perfect except for one by fault; he enjoyed an unsteady life and did not wish to know anything of marriage.

Julien's appearance robbed the social gathering of a lively man who was admired for his elegant storytelling. Herr Von-Rosen became engaged in deep conversation with the widow of his friend and only seldom allowed any interruption from the gathering. Their conversation remained lively right up to the point at which they were forced to part and it was continued on the following morning in the home of the widow.

The content of the conversation was Julien's ghostly apparition. Herr Von Rosen has always been a strong disbeliever in such appearances and, even when her husband was alive was able to explain such ghost stories logically. He disbelieved in the appearance of his dead friend and both party's arguments were fuelled with great passion. So that they could not come to an agreement.

After Herr Von Rosen tried, unsuccessfully, to convince Julien that she was either disturbed by her own senses or due to other people's, that he called out at once
"What if everything could be explained otherwise".
"In an other way perhaps" said Julie "but also better?"
"Who knows? You have not explained the special circumstances of your husbands death to me. He died in a bathing place, in your absence and suddenly!"
"You are shaking your head in doubt. Do you want to perhaps convince me that he did not really die?"
"I don't intend to do anything other than discern an explanation which you may discard if you do not like it."
"And I…" said Julien sentimentally "I would like to ask you not to perform such experiments over the ashes of he whom I held dearest in the whole world."
Herr Von Rosen, who insisted sincerely that he, as the best friend of the deceased, should have the right to explore the details of his death stood up disappointedly, since Julien did not want to provide any explanation, and began searching for his hat.
"It is true…" said Julien "You do indeed have the right to know but I also have the right to warn you against any misuse."
Tearfully the widow told the story, with all its detail, and said, since she could not read his serious facial expression, "And what do you think to such?"
"Not the slightest that you would not want to hear."
"Your shrugging upsets me, Herr Von Rosen. I believe that against so much undoubtful proof of his death there should be no attempt to dare to give any other explanation."
"And am I forbidden by yourself to destroy your belief in this?"
"Herr Von Rosen…" she said to him as he appeared to be ready to leave "I want, I have to listen to you now"
"But then you must allow me to mention circumstances which proceeded the unfortunate event."
"You may mention whatever you deem necessary."
"I am ready. I have heard it in your own words that the relationship between you and your husband, shortly before his death was nothing like the former harmony. So I must suspect that both of you were secretly not against the breaking up of you marriage. A few years earlier all hopes and wishes of your husband were centred upon a big journey. Those wishes were pushed away by his love for you and the luck of being to be able to claim you as his wife. Later circumstances changed again and I suppose this had woken up his old travel lust again and there were only two ways to proceed; either to travel with you or without you. It was a bit too much to expect of you to share all the harshness and difficulty of such a journey in a different part of the world, since you, to be honest, did not even always enjoy his presence. To travel without you would

have meant to expose you to boredom and worry of his return and thus disturbed you in your pleasures. Of those two ways there was none to be taken.

There existed two other methods which would allow a radical separation. One of those was called divorce. But this ugly word upset you husband. It would have caused a lot of talk about you and by those people who, not long ago were annoyed by such unusual gentleness between you. The reproach of your father, who was from the beginning against your marriage would have made your life miserable. That is why this way was also brushed aside. The last option, which will explain itself, appeared strange and adventurous but it promised my friend his freedom and you, after a short period of grief, a second husband more in keeping with your desires"

"Herr Von Rosen" interrupted the widow "You perform as a lawyer during a bad trial. In order to tire out your opponent you try to stretch the story at length by the inclusion of needless detail. I would not want to lose a word of it if you would but avoid mention of those areas of my life which I regret most and which tug most painfully at my heart strings!"

"My truest friend!" said Her Von Rosen "I have already blamed myself for mention of such memories some time ago. But I had to mention those times since they are the necessary foundation of the building which I have half completed."

"But why create such a card-house which the death certificate, which I will show you in a moment, will blow down?"

"The death certificate? As if never before one of those has been issued without a reason! But since I have passed the most difficult areas already please allow me to continue with my hypothesis. Your husband travelled to the bathing place where he met his brother. He mentioned to him his marital problems. He tells him that he would be happy to give away a third of his wealth if he could regain his freedom. The circumstances there were probably that your husband felt pity for those few patients who were not well looked after and his offer of medical support provided the opportunity to buy his freedom. The bad accommodation of one patient was used as an excuse to create a room for him in the same house as your husband shared with his brother. As expected the patient died despite the best care and treatment and your husband left that night to leave all necessary arrangements to his brother. Don't you find my hypothesis now more logical?"

"Not at all. And I am asking you to explain those arrangements in more detail."

"If I do not tire you with such then I shall continue with pleasure. Your husband who, in keeping with the plan, pretended to suffer from illness for a few weeks, left his house clothes behind in which the dead patient was dressed (of whom it was said was getting better and who had then retuned to his home) the dead person was thought to be your husband and buried. So! I think the puzzle is now solved."

"Apart from a few small things which you have left out which demand a certain consideration. An important secret does not need to be shared amongst many if it should not lose its meaning, there you have to agree. But how many know about it?"

"Nobody, apart from the old servant of your husband's brother, whose particular loyalty, as I remember, was mentioned on several occasions in this very room. Whilst on the bathing holiday your husband and his brother had probably only this one servant in attendance and there was no danger that he would expose the secret."

"I have to contradict this in order to release myself from your unfortunately unrealistic and incorrect explanation. You have forgotten quite some facts Herr Von Rosen. A man who had so many friends at the bathing location as my dead husband would have had , undoubtedly, some visitors, even after his death. Friends always wish to see, once more, the beloved remnants when the friend himself has passed over to the other side. And they would have undoubtedly missed his recognisable features when looking at any randomly provided corpse.

"Yes, dearest friend. Even I am convinced that your husbands brother will have had some visits and would have had to give some well thought out explanations. The latter appears to me a quite difficult task which could have only been successful in the hands of a worldly gentleman. I know for sure that many saw the dead body, apart from the face, which was completely disfigured due to a fall out of the bed and therefore covered with linen cloth."

"And the embalmer. Herr Von Rosen? Or do such type of people not exist in a well known bathing location, or do they not have a duty to check upon the natural cause of death?"

"Undoubtedly, such a person and duties exist there but who would suspect that a well respected man would have caused an unnatural death of his brother? For a piece of gold the embalmer would have possibly, taken her duties somewhat lighter and, if asked, agreed not to disturb the facial wounds of the corpse. I do not even have to suspect that the poor dead person fell out of bed resulting in his face becoming unrecognisable or that someone used brutal force after his death to take away any recognition."

"But my dearest Rosen! What have you achieved with such a long and artificial explanation? Or with such twisting of the events?"

"At least the thought of the possibility that your husband is still alive?"

"Only certainty, which your strange explanation does not offer, would give me peace. Eventually you might intend to pursue the argument further and come to the conclusion that it is not an apparition but my supposed dead husband himself who I have seen in my rooms?"

"Unmistakenly, unless you want me to believe in an overactive imagination or the fact that you have been the victim of deceit."

"But why, dearest Rosen, are you trying to be of sharp senses now? The man who according to your explanation paid a third to regain his freedom from me, is the same man who now appears in my home and thus risks his exposure? I have to admit to you that my senses are not sharp enough to understand the connection of such peculiarness."

"The connection is quite obvious. Let us just presume the not unexpectable that your husband who followed his desire to live in a different part of the world and gained pleasure by seeing you satisfied, didn't waste any time to think about anything else initially. And let us even push his regrets away until he achieved his wish. But his regrets had to come, particularly because of his sentimentality. He now admits how hard he had punished you and that it wasn't calculable what consequences his presumed death could have caused despite the disharmony between the two of you. By having those thoughts the happy images of glory of the previous times would have been renewed in his heart. His desire brings him back. He comes here and wishes nothing more than to see you being content. He discovers a method to enter your house and is believed to be a ghost."

"My God!" called the widow "If only you spoke the truth. But unfortunately this explanation is even less likely than that of his death. Everything up to his return might be plausible but why did he have to choose such adventurous night visits?"

"Why? Because he did not know anything of your thoughts and feelings and because he, believed dead, could not dare to be seen by anyone during daylight in a town where even every child knows him."

"And that he entered and left via a closed locked door, how do you explain this?"

"Quite easily. Particularly since you mentioned to me that your less moral but pretty maid has gone to the masked ball that particular night. Could he not have arrived on the same evening and gone to the masked ball to possibly meet you or to gain news in his disguise about you? Could he have not met your pretty maid by chance and due to the informality of the ball become intimate with her? And could he not have given his companion a few glasses of wine too many and thus secretly removed her keys and used them to let himself in to your house. For him, who knows every corner of this house it would not have been difficult to find his way to your chamber even in the darkness."

Julien answered very sentimentally "Much too far fetched, Herr Von Rosen. If you only intended to finish it off with such a bad joke. I am convinced that my dead husband was far too proud a man to let himself in for such a disgraceful adventure as this with my maid. Therefore it pains me to be spoken about him in such a way even after his death."

"But my best friend!" said Rosen "You are getting the wrong end of the stick. By using this example I was only intending to show you but one of many ways in which he *could* have obtained the key which appeared to be so important to you. In the hurry, I agree, I have chosen an untidy example which does not reflect the character of your husband. More likely I could have given him a good friend as a companion who himself was not averse to such a masked ball adventure. Whilst your husband was searching for you, or news about you, could not his companion have met a girl and discovered that she had been your maid and told your husband about it, secretly stolen the keys and retuned them after use to the drunken and unconscious maid without her knowing anything amiss."

"Let's stop here Herr Von Rosen you have managed to present my faults in very bright colours in front of my painful eyes by mentioning those times before my husbands death. And you have put many a possibility before me, with your skill of argument for explaining ghostly appearances, to no purpose. By the way, nobody could convince me that I have seen my actual husband himself in this spectre even though the appearance looked just like my husband. Its gait and it's etheric surrounding, which make me judder, tells me that the wraith belonged to a different world."

"Your Fear, best friend, would have undoubtedly created an etheric atmosphere."

However, Julien disagreed and insisted that the appearance did not have the certainty of human shape.

"Then" continued Herr Von Rosen "Someone must have undoubtedly played an unpleasant trick on you"

"Even so answered Julien the trick could only take on the colour but never the being of the truth."

"You do not know enough of those tricks" said Herr Rosen "But I know how to handle those supposed ghost appearances."

Julie vigorously refused to accept any proof which he offered. He tried forcefully to destroy her belief in the supernatural appearance and thus became more and more adamant. To get rid of him, the widow finally said that she would allow him to do whatever he wanted under the condition that he would not dare to attempt to sway her belief in ghosts. She hid her displeasure of the fact that that she had allowed him to use one of the more distant rooms of the house, with a separate exit, eight days ago, to make his preparations and that he had now put locks on it.

The secret regrets which she had because of the whole thing softened the thought that the whole procedure was not just a joke but the desired wish to remove all doubts. Nevertheless she became noticeably emotional by the black cloth and fancy ceremony with which he attempted to summon the ghost and said to her.

"You see even today when you knew that you have only to deal with a pure deception you couldn't resist such an unusual atmosphere."

"Maybe the ghost who is going to appear has the same etheric cover which you have given to it's particular appearance. Perhaps I should not prevent or destroy a big part of your impression".

Yes I will tell you beforehand in which costume the figure is going to appear to you."

Julien was surprised when he showed her a miniature picture in which her departed husband is presented in the same coat in which he latest appeared in front of her bed and about which she had not spoken to anyone.

"What would you say dearest friend", said Herr Von Rosen, "If instead of the promised hallucination the truth, your husband himself would come out of the room and the explanation, which in your opinion were useless and stupid the latest one from the masked ball excluded, which upsets you most, contain the true story of the real happening what would you say if your husband comes through the door and the details that I told you were true.?"

As Julien's surprise due to Rosen's convincing tone turned into excitement he went slowly towards the door and opened it to reveal the all convincing proof.

The loved ones sunk into each others arms. Rosen himself was the best friend of the doctor of the masked ball and now the man who was supposed to test the feeling of the supposed widow. Dr Hess would have hardly dared to do such if he would not have got hold of the newspaper which contained the ghost story in which he recognized his wife and her passion towards the supposed dead husband despite the falseness of the story.

These events were kept secret from the town in which they happened. Julien sold all her belongings and disappeared and nobody really knew where to. The couple moved to Welschlands where the doctor's brother had made his home in order to recover from an illness. There they lived under the name which doctor Hess had used since his supposed death. And who on seeing the happy couple and knowing the story would wish some other unhappily married couple a similar *Salto mortale* as a cure?

The Grey Room

Last winter secretary Blendau travelled to Italy with his wife the Duchess. They came to a nice town in the North of the land where the Duchess wished to rest for a few days. Blendau asked for, and was allowed to take, this time as a holiday to visit his stepfather, the mayor, who lived six miles away in a Manor house. This was where, until reaching the age of fourteen, Blendau had grown up. It had been seven years since he had left and he had not been back since. He was pleased by the idea of being able to surprise the Mayor and his family.

Since he knew the way Blendau rented a horse. A wonderful winter's morning made the prospect of the reunion even nicer. However after midday the sky became cloudy, and by evening it began to snow heavily. Snowflakes flew in his face and he lost his way. He had hoped to arrive at the Manor courtyard at around five o'clock but it was now really, really dark and his repeater-watch showed eight o'clock. Eventually he reached the county of his fatherly friend and, despite the terrible weather, from here he knew exactly which way to go and so, after half an hour, frozen to the bone and exhausted from the nine mile ride he was happy to finally arrive.

The Mayors wife was in town with her children and only the old father was at home. He hardly recognised the secretary who had grown big and tall. The father wanted to send for his wife and children almost straight away but Blendau asked him not to so that they would be even more surprised when they unexpectedly met him in his room.

The happy father ordered the table to be set with virtually everything that his kitchen had to offer. The old wine soon helped Blendau to recover his strength. They both drunk three small bottles and they talked about the main events in the last seven years of their separated lives. Blendau became more and more tired and was looking forward to having some rest.

"Yes, dear Toby. The old man said. "Don't take it badly my dear Toby that I still call you as you have been called here before. I cannot get used to 'Herr Secretary. Yes, what I wanted to say Toby, is that if you want to sleep then you have to wait until my wife comes back and gives some bed-covers out."

"In the grey room" Brigitte, the parlour maid, interrupted, "is a freshly made bed Mayor. If it suits Herr Secretary."

"No. My Toby would not lay down in there."

"Why not my dearest father?" said Tobias

"In the grey room? Have you already forgotten the castle mistress?"

"Ah, I have not thought of her for a long time. Ha ha ha ha let me sleep up there. Today no ghost will do me any harm. And if the good child will lay next to me in the bed it would not interrupt my sleep as I am so terribly tired."

"Oh Toby, you must have changed a lot because seven years ago you would not, for any price, have spent a night in the grey room. And now you would really have the heart to do so?"

"Without any concerns. Now anyway. I have been five years in the town and there you get a different understanding about such things."

"Well then. I do not have anything against it Toby. Lay down in Gods name. Brigitte light the way to the grey room for Herr Secretary"

Tobias said goodnight and asked again for the Mayor not to mention his arrival to his wife and children for he wanted to surprise them tomorrow at breakfast. He went with the girl up two flights and along the upstairs corridor. The last room of this deserted wing was the grey room. Brigitte set the candles under the old rustic oval mirror. The girl felt scared in the big grey chamber and hurriedly retreated through the door.

Tobias looked around. Everything was as it had used to be in the old grey mysterious room; the huge iron heating stove with 1616 engraved upon it; the door with the little round church windows in the long dark passageway that led toward the prison tower; the six decrepit stools; the two tables with slate tops and carved deer feet and the wide four poster bed with heavy silky gilt laced drapes. Everything was still the same as it had probably been one hundred years ago, ever since the Mayor's family, as long as anyone could remember, had owned the property. However, older than anything was the unfortunate castle girl, Gertrude, who does not rest peacefully in her grave. She had, it had been said, sworn her virginity to heaven and was due to cover her beauty behind the veil of the nunnery when Graf Hugo arrived to satisfy his lust. It was in this very grey room that he broke that gentle rose. She swore by the cross to have called for help; alone far away from the main body of the castle who could have heard the cry of the innocent. Despite being raped she did not become pregnant but in confession the girl told one of the priests that she was robbed of her virginity. He closed the doors to the temple in front of her and told her that she had to suffer the agonies of purgatory for three hundred years.

She died in the grey room from a secretly taken poison at the age of nineteen.

Since then she has been haunting the room and there remains another forty years as decreed by the judgemental priest. Blendau had often heard the tale of Gertrude. Many swore that they had actually seen the castle ghost. They all agreed that she had a crucifix in one hand and a dagger in the other; probably to stab Hugo, the black Graf, and to become reconciled with heaven. Her appearances were only noticed in the grey room and so, for a long time, this room had remained unlived in. Only since the Mayor took over the castle had the room been furnished as a guestroom, but, strangely enough, no guest had liked to stay in it for no one had slept in it peacefully.

Cousin Tobias looked around, making the point that he did not actually believe in the ghost any more, no longer seemed to make much sense.

He closed the door through which he and Brigitte had come and bolted the windowed door to the prison tower. He put one light out and took the other to the bed. He lay down, commended his soul to the Lord, put the second light out, dove under the soft eiderdown and slept like a dead man.

But his sleep did not last long. After two hours he woke; with closed eyes he heard the tower bell chime twelve. He opened his eyes and saw light in the room. He straightened up in the bed. The shock made him wide awake. His gaze fell through the bed-drapes towards the mirror. There, the castle-ghost Gertrude stood in her funeral-shroud with the crucifix in her left hand and a big flashing steel-dagger in the right hand. Blendau was quite awake. He saw with clear eyes. The blood cooled in his veins. This was no story, no dream, this was the terrible truth. The castle-ghost was sumptuous but pale. In her hair she wore the corpse's wreath of rosemary and sequin-gold. He heard the sequin-gold rustling; he heard the funeral-shrouds' rustles; he saw his light burning before the mirrors; he saw the shining stare of her eye; her pale lips. He wanted to get out of the bed and go out of the little door through which he and Brigitte had come. But he could not move a limb because of the shock.

The corpse of the unhappy suicide victim kissed the cross and prayed quietly. Blendau saw the movement of the arsenic lips and the eyes directed up to the heavens. She lifted the Steel dagger towards heaven and, staring terribly, turned towards the bed and, with her white funeral-shroud rustling, came directly towards him.

He was no longer strong. His pulse was still. The wraith bent the drapes of the four-poster bed back and as she saw a man in her bed her cold starry eye shot him a horrible gaze. Suddenly the castle-ghost lunged the dagger towards the breast of the supposed Hugo. At that moment a poison drop from Gertrude's hand fell onto Blendau's face. Frightened he cried out loud. He collected his last strength together and sprang out of bed towards the window to shout for help.

But the woman caught up with him as he fled. She lay her hand against the window so that he could not open it and with the other embraced him. He screamed out loud again, because he had felt the coldness of death down his whole spine as she filled her grave-silent arms with him. It was deathly cold.

She had neither cross nor dagger anymore in the hand. His life seemed to be no longer her goal, but something still more horrifying, his love. The ice-cold phantom embraced him but an almost three hundred year old spirit could not warm him and he froze in her arms.

He wound free and threw himself against the small door; there a skeleton stood: with the right hand, it held the handle, with its' small head, it grinned directly into his face. The skeleton – the hideous shape of Count Hugo –
seemed to have just entered via the small doorway. It pulled the door closed behind itself. A immense noise boomed through the whole house. The ghastly skeleton threw itself upon Blendau; Gertrude sank to the floor, the lights went out and Blendau escaped into the bed pulling the blanket over his ears.

He didn't move; the whole room was deadly quiet; it soon became warm under the covers, sweat broke out from every pore. But he dared not at any price move his head from under the blanket. Eventually nature was stronger and he fell asleep.

It was dawn when he awoke. It was as if he lay in water. His whole bed was wet. Eventually he dared to move his head out from under the covers. His first thought was to believe that the night had been a terrible dream. He forced himself to believe it.

However, he noticed the candle, which he knew for certain that he had put out by the bed, stood on the table under the mirror; and as he saw, that both the candles that had barely half burned due to him putting them out in the evening were now a lot less than half left now. The belief that it had just been a dream dwindled .The truth stood whole and hideous in front of his very soul.

He could tell no-one in the house of this appearance. The family, that had so often teased him in his youth with his fearfulness, would have tortured him half to death; for none of them really believed in the existence of the young suicide lady. Or, if he, through holy and well meant insistence so ruined the whole house's peace then who could live in the castle in which the pale Gertrude with the ghastly skeleton of black Hugo regularly relived her adventure? If he said nothing, then he had future nights to sleep in the suicide room, in the grey room, and he was not keen to do so.

He dressed quickly, hurried to the stable, mounted his horse and, without saying goodbye to the sleeping family, he left and in the same evening was again by his wife.

His full conviction that some unnatural ghostly scene occurred was bolstered by the fact that he was adamant that both doors of the room were still solidly bolted. Blendau, a conscientious and most reliable young man, guarantees every word of this story with his honour; with his life.

With the continuation of his trip to Italy Blendau also came through my domicile. We were old friends. He visited me. We chatted through the winter-evening by a bowl of punch. He told me the full terribleness of his Night in the grey room. At first I laughed in his face; I had myself, in earlier times, heard of the castle-ghost but, naturally, never believed in her. Meanwhile, as he swore
upon our old friendship, that not a syllable of the whole story was made up I decided to quietly get to know Fraulein Gertrude personally. This I could do quickly, since I knew the Mayor well from earlier times and had business in his area that necessitated my presence.

Early this year, I started my little trip. The Mayor offered me his hospitality. He actively remembered me from old times and since he had heard that I was in the vicinity asked me to remain by them, and, to arrange to conduct all my business from there. I accepted his suggestion with thanks. I had arrived in the morning and after lunch, the constable reported, that the big dam was broken through and that the stream had flooded the whole village. The father and the son got on their horses, the mother and Lottchen, went up the stairway with me, to watch the water from a higher window. Lottchen opened a door, we stepped into a big room; it was the grey room. Blendau's description had been picture perfect. Even the two half burned candles, from that terrible night, still stood on the table, under the mirror!

Had I not been too ashamed of myself I would have happily backed out of the decision to sleep there. Even on a bright day the big grey room had something recoiling: and how much more by night! God knows, what it might have been. For what purpose had this large arched chamber been made on the third floor? - However, I had come, to stand up to the pale Gertrude.

I said therefore in the room.

"Obviously your guest-room?" I asked as I directed my gaze towards the guest-bed.

"Only when we have so many guests that we can not let you stay downstairs." the mother replied. "Guests usually stay with us below."

"Oh, please allow me to sleep up here. I love the big room, you can really move about in it."

"You would not like it up here" said the pretty Lottchen as she threw her mother a meaningful look.

"Why not, Miss? The view here is wonderful; my pipe here by the window early in the morning – I can think of nothing more delightful".

"My daughter meant only" interrupted the Mayoress, fixing her daughter with a stern look, "that you would not like it because the room does not heat well and it gets smokey with changing winds but the view is really good. You can see as far as four miles on bright days. If you wish I will bring your things up here."

Admittedly I asked for the room again but the exchange of glances between mother and daughter were not without meaning.

I was now worried about the night. Something was the matter. Blendau had not had a dream. The broken Dam steered our conversation to the flood. The stream had spread long and wide so that it formed a lake of at least a mile square. The evening sun mirrored itself in the floodwater which now surged on its wide new bed; quieter than I could imagine sleeping in my four-poster bed this night.

The sons came back with their father. We spent the evening drinking coffee, chatting and playing. I willingly drank a few glasses of wine. I was shaking a little bit. I had to warm myself from within. But it did not seem to work. I was unable to keep the cold feeling at bay.

Do not sneer at me dear readers! Just go alone to that remote vault and, you can lie as much as you like, you would prefer to sleep close to people that you know and in a friendly room than up there, in the big cold bed where perhaps Gertrude died from poison.

An hour after the evening meal we went our separate ways. The father and sons said in surprised unison "So?" when they heard that I had asked for the grey room. This fatal, 'So?', on the lips of such a wise man and two younger men, almost took my breath away. I was at the point of asking for an explanation for this 'So?' and to tell the family of Blendau's scary appearances in the accursed grey room. But what caused Blendau to refrain from speaking of the matter also caused me to remain silent.

I had not seen with my own eyes, had not heard with my own ears. If anyone doubted the truth of Blendau's story then I would not have anything with which to contradict and prevent my friend's embarrassment. If there was no doubt in the story then I might reinforce the whole of their fear of Gertrude and might cause everyone who still lives peacefully in this building to leave. Therefore I remained silent. I purposefully did not mention one syllable of Blendau's name. What should I say when they heard that I had seen him not long ago and they ask me why he rode away without seeing them first. I acted as if I did not know that Blendau existed.

Brigitte lit the way for me. As I wished the family goodnight, almost all of the family exchanged knowing glances. Only the mother looked at each of them, one after another, with a furtive glance.

As a joke I asked Brigitte to keep me company. I would be a bit lonely up there.

"Here in the grey room?" said the girl as she lit Blendau's candle from the one she had brought. "No, and you could give me a thousand guineas, I would not sleep up here".

"Now, what does the room do? It is a room like any other."

"If you want company you can have it soon. It might come without invitation. Good night dear Sir" And with that, the small thing left via the door. One could see that she was afraid.

I was now in the big decrepit room alone. Still, I was reasonably prepared. I took off my keenly sharpened sabre and my trusty pistols. I poured fresh gunpowder into my pistols and laid my weapons on the stool by the bed. I filled my pipe but the tobacco did not seem to taste right. The faraway roar of the flood and the simultaneous continual groaning swinging and ticking of the pendulum from the nearby clock tower provided me with a bit of atmosphere. The first groaning sounded so wild, so damning; the latter ticking like the picking of a gigantic feeding grave-worm.

I took the light and a pistol and searched the whole room; I searched for secret doors, for trapdoors out in the hall; I searched the bed and underneath it. The table beneath the mirror was covered with drapes; I opened them; I felt overall with my hand to see if there was a hairspring; a lock; a hidden hinge. I found nothing remotely suspicious. My bed had white covers. I closed the window carefully, bolted both doors, first the small curved door, through which Brigitte and I had come then the large glass paned door. Unfortunately when bolting the latter I looked through the pane into the long passage that led to the prison-tower beyond. – God in heaven, there in the passageway stood the hideous skeleton, the Black Count, big and terrifying with an old knights-sword in his bony hand.

My hair stood on end. The shock, rather than courage, caused my reaction. I pulled myself together, quickly unbolted the door, sprang out and screamed like a person possessed:

"Count Hugo, the last dance with me."

I raised my pistol, pulled the trigger – it did not work. The skeleton lifted the sword, the skull grinned, I fled. I threw the pistol away and dived back into the grey room, bolted the door behind me and threw myself into bed.

There, I lay in the same bed that - according to what Blendau had told me - Gertrude had died from poisoning; in the same bed that no human being could sleep quietly and in that which my friend Tobias had sweated.

I left the light burning. The second loaded pistol lay on the stool by my bed.

I lay for a long while. At first an uncontrollable shiver shook me, then – wait – what was that? Something shuffled slowly, like a giant's foot on thinly spread sand. I listened! Again I pulled my senses together. I grabbed the sabre for I could not depend upon the damned pistols. With both hands gripping the sabre I sat up in bed having decided to wait for whatever came.

A hellish laughter resounded from the passageway; a man and a woman's voice; Hugo and Gertrude.

Just like Blendau I stuck my head under the covers, lay my sabre near me and prayed for my soul. After two hours I fell asleep.

In the morning I awoke. My light had burnt out. I had apparently slept. Alone in the room I was no longer disturbed by anyone.

I dressed quickly and hurried to the living room of the Mayor, where the family had gathered together for breakfast.

I needed information; I had to know if the people in this house knew anything about the previous confounded couple. I told them the experiences of Blendau and myself. They almost burst themselves laughing.

Lottchen, the roguish child, had thought up the farce. Actually the whole thing had been meant for Tobias. I came into the story by accident.

Tobias Blendau had been the victim in the house. The children of the Mayor had played thousands of tricks on him. The grey room had always been the centre of his fears. One could have offered him a million; he would never go in the grey room. Then he came back after seven years. He spoke of his growing understanding, from his time of improved enlightenment etc. He told all this to the father of the family, and on the arrival of his cousins, he seemed to be a completely different person. That is where Lottchen got the great idea to test him.

The two brothers had to help the new Gertrude. The parents, naturally, knew not a word about the mischief. Lottchen was counting on Tobias' well known deep sleep. When Cousin Tobias had a busy day then one could set off a signal cannon, he would not wake up. On this day he had made a long and arduous ride: He certainly slept quite deeply. She sneaked to the glass door. He was really snoring, like a Boulton and Watt steam engine. There was a broken round pane in the glass door through which Lottchen could unbolt the door; with stockinged feet she went in and then unbolted the curved door, got a skeleton, which her father had used in earlier times to teach human anatomy, placed it by the curved door which was slightly ajar, lit both candles with the lantern that she had brought and organised it so that Fritz stood outside by the curved door. Karl hid under the table in-front of the mirror and Lottchen, dressed in a very hastily stitched funeral-shroud and a death wreath in her hair, she had also powdered her face and chest. As it was about to strike twelve, standing in-front of the mirror she placed a crucifix in her left hand and a big, long icicle in the right. Now she made a loud noise and Blendau woke up.

The drops of poison that fell onto Blendau's face from Gertrude's hand had been pure water from icicle in Lottchen's hand.

The ice-cold hands with which she embraced Blendau's back were naturally the hands that had become cold and wet as they held the icicle that Lottchen had meanwhile put under the pillow in Blendau's bed.

The skeleton did not close the door behind itself, instead Fritz pushed it powerfully closed; that was the reason for the terrible bang and therefore drawing the skeleton out of the shadow by the door where Blendau stood.

Shortly before she sank to the ground Lottchen grabbed the light and put it out. As Blendau went to the curved door Karl crawled out from under the table and, as Lottchen put out her light, he blew out the candle.

Blendau dived back into bed. All three did not move until, after approximately an hour, Tobias began to snore again. Quietly they took the skeleton out of the room, put everything back in its place, bolted the curved door went out via the glass-door and bolted it again using the broken pane. The three glasses of wine that he had had might also have contributed to Blendau's nightmare.

Accidentally, Blendau had mentioned to the Mayor, before that frightening night, that he was also going to visit me. They knew Blendau's talkative nature, he had probably told me, as a friend, about the happenings in the grey room. When I arrived, not mentioning Blendau but asked to sleep in the grey room the playful adults guessed my game. Lottchen did not feel bad about making me into a second Tobias. But as they saw me bringing pistols and a sabre to my room they lost a little courage. Even before my ghost apparatus had been noticed the damned skeleton had been put in the passageway so as to be close at hand in the night.

Brigitte joined in the pact. My pistol rendered useless because Karl poured water in them. They all denied lifting the sword in the skeletons hand; my shaken imagination must have caused me this deception.

All three had shuffled on the sand spread in the passageway: they sneaked to the glass door and as they found me sitting in bed with the sabre they all laughed out loud. That was the hellish laughter. They could not take the joke any further otherwise their parents would have read them the riot act because of Blendau's torment.

Lottchen's rosy lips eventually had to atone. I kissed the blushing Gertrude until she swore an oath never to tease anyone else in the grey room.

But the parents would not let me sleep up there again because the rats and mice are so lively in the chamber that all visitors that must by chance sleep in the grey room cannot usually close their eyes, even though they are not embraced so tightly by the god Morpheus.

The Black Chamber

Our journal club contained three people, Actuary Wermuth who commented upon the intellectual pages, town physician Bärmann who commented upon the cultural pages and myself who commented upon that which was neither intellectual nor cultural or both together. As well as these gatherings we have meetings and meals together like other journal clubs, but we were even better than the others because we had daily meetings and meals as soon as the actuary had finished with his clients and the town physician his patients. They would come to my house and read the newest from literature and commented upon it whilst enjoying a jug of beer and a pipe of tobacco.

This time, the actuary made us wait longer than usual. After waiting a quarter of an hour we decided to start our literary discussions without him. The newest *Allgemeine* news-sheet already lay on the table and the grey envelope containing the *The Independent* had just arrived in the post. We had no time to waste. I grabbed the news-sheet that belonged to my category and began to read.

The first side contained a direct reproach of the *The Independent*, because of the '*Grey room*'. I read with secret joy, because I had already argued earlier with the town physician about the *Grey room* and had hoped, with this ally in my hand, to knock his belief in ghosts on the head.

"I have long been surprised that the *The Independent*," I said, "which normally sticks to reality and which, on top of everything can have the explanation first hand in Berlin, should take such a thing and turn their paper into, as it were, a piece of obscure propaganda. I am now curious as to how it will justify itself."

"How?" the town physician suggested, "With the silence that it's competition deserves."

And with that he threw himself back in his chair and drew so strongly on his pipe that pipe and mouth both steamed like volcanoes.

"But, I ask you," I began "who should believe such a thing as the wandering dead skeleton and the mad Gertrude, who can touch and light candles, like any normal bodied chamber maid."

"But, I ask you" replied he somewhat heatedly "who should then believe, that you academics alone have all the wisdom and can look upon nature's hand and explain what Nature can or cannot do. You chatter and chatter and the less you understand the situation the louder you speak against it."

He stuffed his finger into his pipe so violently that the head fell of and the glimmering ash fell on the chair.

"Pardon!" he continued as he brushed the chair off, "Don't take it too badly they always use worse and worse clay for the pipes. Yes. What I really want to say, good friend, is that you, as School-manager, do not have the opportunity to become so knowledgeable about nature and it's powers as us doctors. Just believe me, we know so little from what Nature can or cannot do and how it causes something, that – that – ".

"That it is not understandable how to cure a common cold comes to mind."

"Why then do you believe that we can?" was his repost. "Why do you send for us from miles away and consult us and give your belief and money. There you have it. You believe what you want to believe and that which is the most convenient. You do this in morals in politics and in everything. Have not you imprisoned people only because they claimed that the enemy won the battle? The enemy really came into your country and won the battle, and so come ghosts into your house even if you chase all the doubts away."

"I should almost believe," I said, shaking my head, "That you have seen ghosts once yourself".

"So! I don't want to to be known as a ghost–seer but something similar to what happened to Blendau in the Grey room, happened to me and funny enough my bedroom was called the Black Chamber."

Now there was no way back. The town physician had to talk about the Black Chamber. After a short hesitation he re-filled his pipe and forbade anyone to laugh and began:

"I had finished my medical university studies and, in order to gain more experience and acknowledgement, I assisted Dr Wendeborn for a few years. He had the practice with the best reputation. As I was known as a good rider he left me mainly with all the house visits and made his older days more comfortable. Sometimes he sent me to a nearby castle to visit the Colonel von Silberstein whose daughter suffered from a dreadful nervous complaint. There was not much that could be done but I prescribed medicines and diet as demanded by the circumstances. I was keen to take my leave but her parents would not let me go although I left my instructions in writing so that there would be no confusion possible about the treatment of the patient. I had to stay. The women of the house quickly arranged for a room to be made ready for me. As the patient calmed down a bit I retreated, as soon as I could, to my room.

The castle was fairly dark and my little chamber was not the friendliest. The old heavy doors were painted black as was the ceiling and its' old beams. Below the windows, upon the walls, there was also black panelling. To cut the story short I liked nothing about the chamber other than the snow-white covered bed which stood at the wall behind heavy green silk drapes.

I now prepared an in depth report, about the patient's illness, for my senior colleague, and I yawned with every comma. Then, something knocked on my door. I jumped slightly but quickly regained my composure and I called, as abrupt as I could "Come in!" This time it was not anything to worry about, the colonel's hunter wanted to enquire whether I still required anything. I am telling you every tiny detail, on purpose since you have to be exact in such descriptions; just as pedantic as a *Visum Repertum*.

The hunter was a pleasant young man. We talked about this and that and he asked me whether I felt too lonely in the chamber. He offered to stay with me. I laughed as he himself appeared very frightened in the dark chamber. He looked around at every corner with worry and concern at the slightest noise. Eventually he told me that my room was called the Black Chamber, and that there were many unusual tales concerning it though people rarely spoke about them for fear of spoiling a guests' stay. He also told me many a ghostly tale and again offered to stay with me or to share his bedroom, which was much friendlier than this one, with me. I did not want to accept any of his suggestions that would compromise my heartiness. He saw that my resolution was unmoveable so finally he went, stopping in the doorway to repeat his warning against the attitude of disbelief which had spoilt the stay for others.

I was now alone in the notorious black chamber. Back then, when I still thought lightly of ghosts, - like knowledgeable people, I believed this an opportunity to prove my heroism and looked forward to midnight.

First I examined my room in detail. I closed both doors and barred them from inside with a special lock. I did the same with the windows. With my travelling sabre I poked about under the bed and all around the table and cupboards. Only, when I was sure that it was impossible for me to be surprised by either man or beast, did I get undressed. I put my nightlight in the stove so that my room was completely dark because scant illumination creates more fear than the darkness that it should free one from.

After these preparations I lay down and, as I had hoped, because of my earlier tiredness, was soon asleep. I had only just got to sleep, so it seemed, when I heard my name whispered. I pulled myself together and listened, again I heard clearly the call "August!" The sound came, it seemed, from the drapes of my bed. I opened my eyes wide but saw nothing but thick darkness around me. Meanwhile the call had sent a chill down my spine. I shut my eyes tightly and, again, began to slumber. All at once a noise in the drapes woke me and the calling of my name came to me even clearer. I half opened my eyes, my room seemed to me to have changed; it was illuminated by a wonderful light, an ice-cold hand touched me and next to me, in bed, lay a pale dead shape in a funeral-shroud, it's cold arm reaching out for me. I screamed out aloud with the initial shock and bounced back, there was a sudden bang, the shape was gone and I saw nothing around me except the previous darkness. I pulled the blanket over my head, the tower clock struck and I counted, it was midnight.

Suddenly I recollected myself and jumped out of bed without delay to make sure that no dream could have given me a false impression. I lit two lights and, as before, searched the whole room. Everything was just the same as I had left it. No bolt on the door had been displaced, no window-latch moved. I was almost tempted to blame this appearance upon a dream and vivid fantasies that were brought to life due to the stories of the hunter. However, upon completing my examination, I was shining light upon my bed and there, on my pillow, lay a long lovely dark lock of hair. It could not have come out of a dream or an illusion. I picked it up and was just about to write down the occurrences of this night when I became aware of a distant noise. I could suddenly discern fearful running and slamming of doors and then the sound came towards my room and something was hammering forcefully and hastily against my door. I called "Who's there!"

From outside came the answer

"Get up quickly Mr Bärman. The young lady is going to die".

I dressed as quick as I could and raced to the room of my patient. It was too late. The young lady was lying in front of me and her soul had already departed. Just before midnight, it was said, she woke from her sleep and after a few gasps she passed away. The parents were so devastated they now needed my medical support; especially the mother who was not able to leave the corpse so that I had to almost separate her with brute force. Finally she gave in but I had to allow her to take a lock of hair from her daughters head as a relic and memory. Just imagine how I shuddered as I recognised her hair as that which I had discovered in the night.

The day after I was seriously ill and suffered from the same illness from which my patient passed away."

"What do you say to this happening whose occurrence I can swear by every oath on?"

"It is indeed strange" I answered, "If you would not speak so seriously and if you had not reassuredly searched the whole room upon the smallest detail, I would almost have some doubts."

"Like I said to you" said the town physician "Illusion was impossible. I have seen and heard with fully awakened senses and the lock of hair removes all doubt"

"Even so, I have to admit to you" I answered, "I take exception to the lock of hair. If your experience was not an illusion then it must have arisen from your mental state, or however you want to call it, but this becomes rather doubtful due to the appearance of a physical lock of hair.

A ghost that leaves part of its body behind seems to me very suspicious and gives me the same impression as an actor who improperly falls out of character"

The town physician moved on his stool impatiently. "God honor me the consequence!" he called " First you don't believe in ghosts at all and now you have a theory of ghostly character traits and criticise the appearance!"

Now the Aktuarius entered, mopping his brow.

"Probably came from the theatre!" we shouted towards him and rattled the penitence box under his nose.

"Oh! Your having a nice chat then!" he answered sarcastically "Why don't you sit and cross examine petty criminals, vagabonds and other social misfits from the early morning through the whole day? Yesterday there was a couple brought in which cost me a fair bit my lungs."

"In God's name!" said the physician "stay away with all your petty vagabond and criminal stories. We have already argued for over an hour about *The Grey Room* and the Advertiser and Independent newspapers are yet to read."

"I have now a contra to add to the Grey room" added the Aktuarius "You can send it to the *Independent*, when you want, under the title 'The Black Chamber'"

"The Black Chamber?" we both cried, the town physician and I, but each in a different tone.

"Yes, Yes!" repeated the Aktuarius "Listen, a brilliant scoundrel and ghost story"

"Now I am curious" murmured the town physician and drummed upon the table with his fingers.

"You know of course" the Aktuarius began "The lawyer Tippel? – the little buffoon who always flutters around the women – you must know him!"

"Yes, of course, yes!" we both cried "get to the point!"

"Now", he began "he had recently been out in Rabenau on an appointment for the Silberstein courts. The business took quite some time and it was shortly before evening before he was finished. He is, as you know, from nature not the bravest and the tales of highwaymen and tongue-cutters had made him so worried that no-one could persuade him, with any promise in the world, to spend a night on the road. The Silbersteins are good people and because they saw his fear they offered him somewhere to spend the night at the castle. Tippel accepted with much gratitude and apologised in advance for any noise that he might make since he would have to leave at dawn. The next morning though no one heard or saw Tippel. After another hour has passed they knocked on his door, they called, they made a noise: nobody answered. Eventually they decided to force open the door. There lay Tippel deathly white and unconscious in bed and looked as if he wanted to pass away. Eventually, with lots of persuasion, he came round and babbled about terrible things that he had seen in the night.

He had gone to bed early so that he would be able to leave really early in the morning. As soon as he fell asleep he was awakened by a knocking on the door. Since Tippel's head had been filled with fearful tales he pressed himself closer to the wall and stuck his head under the bed-covers. No sooner than he had got back to sleep was he awoken by a new dull rustling on his bed and when he looked he saw a white figure standing in front of a cupboard that he had never seen in the room before. The inside of the cupboard glittered like gold, silver and jewels. The ghost counted it's wealth again, jingled the gold, closed the cupboard and eventually drew nearer to the bed. Tippel saw a small pale corpse-like face wearing an old fashioned head-scarf tied around its black hair. An ice cold wind blew upon him and the ghost looked as if it was about to throw off its mildewy and blotchy grave-clothes and to share the bed with Tippel. Fearing for his life Tippel turned over, closed his eyes tightly and moved as close to the wall as he could. Suddenly there was a loud cry and such a hefty bump close to him that he lost consciousness. That is how he lay, until early morning when, as I have told you, he was found, half dead in bed, by the family.

You could easily imagine how such an event caused a lot of attention. The Silbersteins, who often have this vision anyway, talked about an old Aunt who is supposed to have shown herself before and of walled up treasures which a dowser had indicated to the previous castle's owner. Tippel reassured his hosts that every single word of his story was true and that he would swear to it on oath. Indeed he went so far as to leave an affidavit upon the matter with the local courts and the sceptical justice of the peace insisted upon a local inspection of the room where Tippel had slept. The old Silberstein was not keen on this as he did not want to get in touch with any ghosts in his house. He could easily spare the black chamber and would be happy if the ghost would be satisfied with this.

The Justice of the peace was a determined man and over-ruled the wish of Silberstein, so the Black chamber was opened. Tippel could not quite say where the cupboard with the treasure had stood because opposite the bed were only windows and there was no space where a cupboard, visible or invisible, could have stood. They inspected the complete narrow chamber but could not find the tiniest trace of anything suspicious or ghostly anywhere. The Justice of the Peace and those who watched proved undoubtedly that there was no logical explanation for what happened. Tippel asked for a certified copy of the findings and his own statement so that he could present himself in all newspapers as a genuine, certified, witness to ghostly events.

At this point the Justice of the Peace decided to examine the bed in which Tippel had slept. He shook, rattled and poked in and around the bed. Suddenly, the panelled wall behind the bed slid upwards exposing the bed in the next room, through whose drapes it was possible to see into a really beautiful room.'

'Oh my goodness!' exclaimed the town physician and slapped himself on the forehead with the palm of his hand.

The Aktuarius did not understand the reaction of the town physician and continued. 'That is just how Tippel reacted when the second room was discovered. The witnesses crawled over the beds and into the adjoining room. Tippel inspected the cupboard of his ghost and the others inspected the chamber maids' room. The cupboard was opened but was not, as Tippel claimed to have seen, full of Jewels, gold and silver but there were some pretty pieces of silver jewellery and money in it. The pretty occupant of the chamber was called for to explain the discovered treasure and nightly appearances, but she, and the young gamekeeper, had disappeared.'

'With the gamekeeper?' exclaimed the town physician.

'With the gamekeeper August Leisegang.' the Aktuarius confirmed.

'August is the trickster's name?' interrupted the town physician 'Do you know this for sure?'

'Why should I not know this?' replied the Aktuarius somewhat annoyed, 'I have just cross examined the gamekeeper and his girl. What is so remarkable about the name?'

'My cousin.' mumbled the town physician fiddling with his collar 'Just continue with your story.'

'Now the rest you guess' continued the Aktuarius 'The sliding panel, which in ancient times served the castle owner some purpose, had been forgotten until being discovered and used by the couple of lovers. Tippel had, whilst asleep, pushed upon a hidden spring, and the wall slid up. This was the noise which had awoken him, the chamber girl had cried out when she saw the stranger in her bed instead of the gamekeeper. She then made the panel drop down and this was the bump that caused tipple to lose consciousness. Now everything explained itself logically. Wanted posters of the couple were put up and yesterday they were brought in by the authorities. I have been sitting since yesterday morning, and cross examining them. The most fun was when Tippel suddenly arrived and was furious when he saw the pretty, rosy cheeked, black-haired girl who he had mistook for a deathly pale miser who had caused him to hide beneath the bedcovers. Tippel said that such should not happen to him again and in order to make up for the missed opportunity of a kiss on that night, he pursed his lips and leant forward but the young chambermaid turned so quickly that Tippel's lips landed upon the red nose of the court usher.'

"Watch yourself!" she said "The first of April comes around every year and will have it's rights every time."

"But" he closed as we finished laughing "even if I have given away to you the secrets of the *Black Chamber*, the *Grey Room* you will not argue away...and now to the papers."

He grabbed hold of the *Independent*.

"*The Grey Room*" he shouted "That is an old piece."

We looked at it. The date was new. The physician read. But before he came to the end he threw the paper on the table as it contained nothing other than the clear solution to the criticized and disputed wonder of the *Grey Room*.

"My Goodness" he shouted we are living in a bad time! Everything old goes to ground, not once a honest ghost can keep himself. Do not come to me again with a ghost story.

"Beware" we both answered "As soon as it is the end with ghosts the right time starts for stories. Every story follows some sort of reality and the reader, with some luck, may discover the truth beneath."

Searching for the muse

A great deal has been written about the events that led to the moment when Mary Shelley first conceived her 'hideous progeny' but the exact events that occurred at the Villa Diodati on the shores of Lake Léman, have become shrouded by the slowly creeping mists of time. There is no dispute, however, that the major catalyst for the group's decision to attempt to write ghost stories began as a result of reading *'Some volumes of ghost stories, translated from the German into French,[which] fell into our hands.'* (1)

> *'We will each write a ghost story, said Lord Byron; and his proposition was acceded to...I busied myself to think of a story, -- a story to rival those which had excited us to this task. One which would speak to the mysterious fears of our nature, and awaken thrilling horror -- one to make the reader dread to look round, to curdle the blood, and quicken the beatings of the heart.* (2)

The stories read by the group were published in *Fantasmagoriana, ou Recueil d'Histoires d'Apparitions de Spectres, Revenans, Fantômes, etc; traduit de l'aalemand, par un Amateur.* They had been translated, from German, by an anonymous author who we now know to be Jean Baptiste Benoit Eyries

Considering the great influence that these stories had upon Mary Shelley who, fifteen years after reading them, wrote: 'I have not seen these stories since then; but their incidents are as fresh in my mind as if I had read them yesterday' (3) it is surprising that the English translation, produced by Mrs. Sarah Elizabeth Brown Utterson and published anonymously, as *Tales of The Dead*, by London, White, Cochrane & Co. in 1812, remains largely unknown. It was not until 1992 that Mrs. Utterson's translation resurfaced briefly; edited by Professor Terry Hale and published by the former Gothic Society.

A further complication to unravelling the mystery of the stories read by the group at Villa Diodati lies in the fact that not all of the stories that appeared in the English *Tales Of The Dead* were in the original *Fantasmagoriana* whilst others that were present in the French book, and thus read by the group, had been omitted from the English translation. With this edition I have attempted to recreate the original collection of stories in order to satisfy the reader's curiosity as to the source of Mary's inspiration and to enable further academic study of the origins of Gothic and Science-fiction genres in English. Consequently three of the stories presented here are unique in that they appear, for the first time, in the English language.

Fantasmagoriana was, as mentioned in both the 1818 and 1831 prefaces to *Frankenstein,* a collection of stories that had been originally written in German. These stories, written by Johann August Apel and Friedrich Laun (the pen name of Friedrich August Schulze) were published in four volumes of their Gespensterbuch (G.J Göschen, Lepzig 1810 -1813), though Apel's *'Die Bilder der Ahnen'* was first published as early as 1805. Now largely forgotten in Germany, the authors were, in their day, both well known and prolific authors. Apel was a successful playwright whose *Der Freischutz,* published in The *Gespenster Buch,* was adapted into one of Germany's most popular and famous Operas by Carl Maria Friedrich Ernst von Weber.

It is not surprising that the book read by Shelley and the others had it's origins in German literature for, during a flurry of literary activity in the late eighteenth and early nineteenth centuries, German stories, that often originated as folk tales or Kunstmärchen, were being rapidly written down and converted into short stories and even novels. The German Schauerroman and Schauergeschichte was the predecessor to, and a great influence upon, semi-gothic fiction such as Mary Shelley's Frankenstein. Indeed many of the influences for this, somewhat forgotten German genre, were tales of German folklore and adult fairytales, many of which were passed on by word of mouth long before being put into print in various forms. *Frankenstein* can thus be considered as a, then modern, fable that weaves a number of thematic warnings into its plot and borrows much of its structure from Germanic literature.

In the 1831 preface to *Frankenstein* Mary Shelley points out, quite clearly, that her famous 'husband' Percy Bysshe Shelley had nothing to do with the inspiration for the novel, but that it was he who provided the preface to the 1818 issue

> *I certainly did not owe the suggestion of one incident, nor scarcely one train of feeling, to my husband, and yet but for his incitement, it would never have taken the form in which it was presented to the world. From this declaration I must except the preface. As far as I can recollect, it was entirely written by him.* (4)

Mary's suggestion that each 'incident' and 'train of feeling' was her own is an understandable claim. Percy's 1818 preface resulted in initial popular belief that he was actually the anonymous author of *Frankenstein* and, even after acknowledgement of the true author, many have been convinced that he may have had more to do with the text than has been suggested. It seems more likely that Mary was indeed the sole author of the text and that, like many successful creative writers, she drew her ideas and inspiration from a number of sources, some of which, until now, have been relatively hard to trace.

The similarities between key scenes in *Frankenstein* and some of the stories in *Fantasmagoriana* can, at times, seem quite startling and provide evidence for the extent to which these stories probably influenced Mary's writing. If we examine excerpts from *Fantasmagoriana*'s *The Grey Room* we soon discover themes and ideas that are reflected both in Mary's debut novel and, perhaps more tellingly, in her own fanciful description of the genesis of her story.

The scene describing Victor Frankenstein's waking view of the creature that he has created is an interesting example of such influence at work. From Mary Shelley's novel we are given:

> '*by the dim and yellow light of the moon, as it forced its way through the window shutters, I beheld the wretch --the miserable monster whom I had created. He held up the curtain of the bed; and his eyes, if eyes they may be called, were fixed on me*'. (5)

In *The Grey Room* from *Fantasmagoriana* the character Tobias is confronted, as he lays in bed, by what he believes is the ghost of a suicide victim.

> *His pulse was still. The monster bent the drapes of the four poster-bed back, her cold bull's eye shot him a horrible gaze,*

This scene is also echoed in Mary Shelley's 1831 preface:

> '*He sleeps; but he is awakened; he opens his eyes; behold the horrid thing stands at his bedside, opening his curtains, and looking on him with yellow, watery, but speculative eyes.*' (6)

Other elements from the same scene in *The Grey Room* are mirrored by those that appear in *Frankenstein* as Victor, in a disturbed sleep, dreams of his fiancé Elizabeth:

From the grey room:

> '*In her hair she wore the corpse's wreath of rosemary and sequin-gold. He heard the sequin-gold rustling; he heard the funeral-shrouds' rustles; he saw his light burning before the mirrors; he saw the shining stare of her eye; her pale lips.... She lay her hand against the window so that he could not open it and with the other embraced him. He screamed out loud again, because he had felt the coldness of death down his whole spine as she filled her grave-silent arms with him. It was deathly cold. She had neither cross nor dagger anymore in the hand. His life seemed to be no longer her goal,*

> *but something still more horrifying, his love. The ice-cold phantom embraced him but an almost three hundred year old spirit could not warm him and he froze in her arms.'*

And here Victor dreams of meeting Elizabeth in Ingoldstadt:

> *'I slept, indeed, but I was disturbed by the wildest dreams. I thought I saw Elizabeth, in the bloom of health, walking in the streets of Ingolstadt. Delighted and surprised, I embraced her, but as I imprinted the first kiss on her lips, they became livid with the hue of death; her features appeared to change, and I thought that I held the corpse of my dead mother in my arms; a shroud enveloped her form, and I saw the grave-worms crawling in the folds of the flannel. I started from my sleep with horror; a cold dew covered my forehead, my teeth chattered, and every limb became convulsed'* (7)

These are but a few of the literary similarities to be gleaned from just one of the tales within the *Fantasmagoriana* collection. Others can be found, as Terry Hales points out (8), in Mary Shelley's hazy recollection of the 'History of the Inconstant Lover' which is actually Friedrich Laun's *Die Totenbraut* (The Death Bride). Part of the pleasure in preparing this book has been the recognizing the inter-textuality evident between the collection of stories in *Fantasmagoriana*, *Frankenstein* and indeed many other texts which Mary Shelley is known to have read.

Having touched, briefly, upon the literary influences upon Mary Shelley's Frankenstein it would be remiss not to mention the very real and physical influences that undoubtedly played a part in the creation of a novel that has not been out of print for over two hundred years.

The scientific nature of Victor Frankenstein's quest and the challenge that it presented to conservative European religious belief of the day is not so dissimilar from the challenges that real physicians were beginning to present during the Enlightenment period.

It is quite feasible that the manner in which Mary's monster was brought to life in her text was heavily influenced by discussions of galvanism and that these discussions were instigated by Byron's personal physician and friend Dr John Polidori.

As a brilliant medical scholar Polidori may well have attended lectures by Dr William Lawrence in Edinburgh, who caused uproar amongst the Royal College of Surgeons when he suggested that life was not an entity separate and superior to the human body and that creation had nothing to do with God. We also

know, from the diary kept by Polidori at the Villa Diodati, that he talked with Percy Shelley about the 'principles of whether man was to be thought merely an instrument' (9). Percy Shelley would have been an ideal partner for this discussion for he too had something of a medical background during his last two years of study at Eton. In fact both he and Mary attended a public lecture on the medical uses of electricity by André-Jacques Garnerin (10).

Discussions of Luigi Galvani's electrical animation of a murderer's corpse, as lightening crackled across the sky outside, quite probably provided additional inspiration for Mary's literary creation.

One of the more obvious, yet surprisingly little known, influences for *Frankenstein* concerns a ruined castle that bears the same name. This hilltop castle which had existed since the sixteenth century had, by the late seventeenth century, fallen into ruin. It was these ruins that, in part, served as an atmospheric inspiration to a young Johann Goethe the famous German poet who was largely responsible for the Sturm and Drang literary movement in Germany. Under the crumbling ruins of Burg Frankenstein Goethe would read excerpts of his novel *The sorrows of young Werther*.

Percy and Mary were quite conversant with the works of Goethe and it is not inconceivable that it was their knowledge of his literary achievements and a certain enlightened curiosity that drew them towards the decaying buildings perched twelve hundred feet above the countryside and shrouded in encroaching forest.

Interestingly, it is at this point that the links between physical influences and Mary's tremendous literary achievement deepen. Not only was there a castle Frankenstein which the Shelleys probably visited, but there was also a local legend concerning the castle. In all probability, during their visit, Mary, Percy and Claire, may have heard the tale of one of the castle's previous occupants.

Burg Frankenstein had, at one stage, been the home of Johann Conrad Dippel who some consider to be the real Frankenstein.

Johann Dippel was born on August 10th 1673 and grew into a very intelligent young man. By the age of 17 he studied theology and soon added medicine and chemistry to the list. Dipple studied at the university in Giessen, where he registered as Dippel of Frankenstein, but turned out to be something of a rogue student. His thesis was entitled 'De Nihlo' (On nothing) which gave the distinct impression that he felt that he had learned nothing from his university professors; an arrogance aptly portrayed in the character of Victor Frankenstein.

Dippel became something of an alchemist and invented a variety of chemical concoctions such as 'Berliner Blau' a blue powdered dye and 'Dippels elexirum vitae', his own elixir to prolong life, which contained nitroglycerin and was responsible for occasional explosions in the Frankenstein castle tower. Many local tales existed about his alchemistical activities including the suggestion, which may be true, that he experimented with pieces of dismembered corpses.

Frankenstein is not an altogether uncommon name in Germany but it was not until Professor Radu Florescu published *In search of Frankenstein: Exploring the Myths behind Mary Shelley's Monster* that a definite link between the ruins near Darmstadt, Germany and Mary's Novel was openly suggested. Florescu's speculations are intriguing and exciting but based upon no more than local folklore. In Stephen Derwent Partington's review of Professor Florescu's book he suggests that:

> '*should proof of Shelley's knowledge of the Castle Frankenstein and the alchemist Dippel be found in future, a significant contribution to Frankenstein scholarship will have been made; a contribution that might forever lay to rest the Romantic nonsense, instigated of course by Shelley herself, that the novel stemmed entirely from a dream*'. (11)

Though Mary and Claire's journals of their travels through Europe, with Percy, have been a good, though sometimes misleading, source for Frankenstein scholars the fact that some of Mary's journals were 'lost' has, quite naturally, presented considerable difficulties.

In *Burg Frankenstein* Walter Scheele claims that this missing journal is in the hands of a Swedish family who are loath to allow others to view it. Nevertheless, Scheele, explains that:

'Es ist mir jedoch nach langem Hin und Her gestattet worden, eine einzelene kurze passage aus dem Tagebuch zu zitieren, eine passage von 1814 , die dem langern Ratselraten – kannte Mary den Frankenstein oder nich? - endlich ein Ende bereitet:' (12)

'I was granted, after much to and fro, permission to cite a short passage from the journal, a passage from 1814 that finally answers the question – did Mary know about Frankenstein or not?' (12) *Translation*

According to Scheele the journal gives a description of castle Frankenstein in Mary's own words:

> '*The Frankenstein Castle: A monumental building, full of darkness; broken walls, mysterical-mighty in the sobering Novembermist – but wonderful shining under the bright moon. Allowing an amazing country-view over the Rhine-river to the blue mountains on the other side of the river and a church to be seen over the silvershining waters*' (13)

The link between Mary's novel and Johann Dippel is further strengthened by her own connection with the master storytellers Jakob and Wilhelm Grimm. After the death of Mary's mother, Mary's father, Charles Godwin remarried. Through her father's marriage Mary acquired both a stepsister Claire Clairmont and a new stepmother Mary Jane Clairmont. Mary Clairmont was an established writer of children's books and the English translator of Johann Rudolph Wyss' *Swiss Family Robinson*. Her talents of translation were also being used by others. Mary Clairmont was also the translator for the Grimm's fairytales which had first been published in Germany in 1812. In his book *Burg Frankenstein* Walter Scheele discusses the contents of a letter, written by Jacob Grimm to Mary

Clairmont, which few have had access to. In the letter Grimm reports of a:

> *'horror-story that should, under no circumstances be published in the fairy tales collection because it is nothing more than a horrible story. The people who live at the foot of the Frankenstein ruins tell their children stories of the occurrences in and around the castle to frighten them into avoiding the castle and nearby woods during winter evenings.'* (14) *Translation*

According to the story a magician was supposed to have lived at the castle and used parts of corpses from the cemetery in the valley to create a monster which he put in the castle prison. One day in November the monster broke out of the prison, killed his creator and fled into the forest. Today he lives there, alone, an enemy of all people. Because of his loneliness the monster grabs little children who wander alone in the forest and drags them back to his hideaway. There he plays with them until he becomes bored. Then he dips the unfortunate children into boiling water and eats them.

The links between Frankenstein and Konrad Dippel, rediscovered by Professor Florescu have not been popular amongst all scholars. Some consider Florescu's suggestions as a direct attack upon the feminine literary genius of Mary Shelley. As such this essay, with it's inclusion of Scheele's discoveries and comparisons between forgotten German texts and *Frankenstein* will no doubt also be received with mixed feelings. It must be remembered that many Mary Shelley biographers have already shown that Mary often relied upon her own personal experiences to provide ideas and landscapes for her writing. It is not the intention of this essay to discredit the huge literary achievement of an author who was so young and yet so enlightened. However, it is important to remember that great literature tends to be based, in some part, upon physical influences and literary works that preceded it. Writing rarely, if ever, springs purely from the imagination (though Mary Shelley wished her readers to believe this to be the case for *Frankenstein*). None of us live in a vacuum. It is the weaving of all the elements of influence, both imaginative and real, into a work of art that is the literary achievement. To suggest otherwise would be to cheapen the true art of the writer.

References

1. Shelley, M., Author's Introduction to the Standard Novels Edition in *Frankenstein*, Oxford World Classics, Oxford University Press, Oxford, 1998, p.194
2. Shelley, M., Author's Introduction to the Standard Novels Edition in *Frankenstein*, Oxford World Classics, Oxford University Press, Oxford, 1998, p.194-195
3. Shelley, M., Author's Introduction to the Standard Novels Edition in *Frankenstein*, Oxford World Classics, Oxford University Press, Oxford, 1998, p.194
4. Shelley, M., Author's Introduction to the Standard Novels Edition in *Frankenstein*, Oxford World Classics, Oxford University Press, Oxford, 1998, p.197
5. Shelley, M., *Frankenstein*, Oxford World Classics, Oxford University Press, Oxford, 1998, p.39-40.
6. Shelley, M., Author's Introduction to the Standard Novels Edition in *Frankenstein*, Oxford World Classics, Oxford University Press, Oxford, 1998, p.196
7. Shelley, M., *Frankenstein*, Oxford World Classics, Oxford University Press, Oxford, 1998, p.39.
8. Hale, T., *Introduction* in *Tales of The Dead*, The Gothic Society, Kent, 1994, P.13
9. Rossetti, W., *From The Diary of Dr. John William Polidori: 1816, Relating to Byron, Shelley, etc.* located at: http://www.english.upenn.edu/Projects/knarf/Polidori/poldiary.html
10. Fieldman, P., Scott-Kilvert D, Eds. The Journals of Mary Shelley 1814-1844., Baltimore, John Hopkins University Press, 1987.
11. Partington, S.D., Review of Radu Florescu, *In Search of Frankenstein: Exploring the Myths behind Mary Shelley's Monster.* located at: http://users.ox.ac.uk/~scat0385/florescu.html
12. Scheele, W., Burg Frankenstein (Mythos, Wahrheit, Legende), Societäts Verlag, Frankfurt am Main, 2001, p.98
13. Scheele, W., Burg Frankenstein (Mythos, Wahrheit, Legende), Societäts Verlag, Frankfurt am Main, 2001, p.98
14. Scheele, W., Burg Frankenstein (Mythos, Wahrheit, Legende), Societäts Verlag, Frankfurt am Main, 2001, pp. 101-102.

Selected Bibliography

1. Apel, J, & Laun, F., *Gespenster Buch*, Insel Verlag, Frankfurt am Main, 1992.
2. Botting, F., *Gothic*, Routledge, London, 2003.
3. Florescu, R., *In Search of Frankenstein*, New English Library, London, 1997.
4. Hale, T., (Ed.), *Tales of The Dead*, The Gothic Society, Kent, 1994.
5. Scheele, W., *Burg Frankenstein (Mythos, Wahrheit, Legende)*, Societäts Verlag, Frankfurt am Main, 2001.
6. Scheele, W., *Märchenhafter Frankenstein*, Societäts Verlag, Frankfurt am Main, 2004.
7. Seymour, M., Mary Shelley, Pan Macmillan, Oxford, 2000.
8. Shelley, M., *Frankenstein*, Oxford World Classics, Oxford University Press, Oxford, 1998, p.39.

fantasmagoriana.com

Selected bibliography

Printed in Great Britain
by Amazon